The Christmas Pact

From festive flings to forever love…?

When their parents shockingly announce they plan to spend Christmas on a month-long cruise, single sisters—and best friends!—Sienna, Thea and Eliza Kendall decide to shake things up for themselves too. The idea? Each sister will organize a surprise trip for one of her siblings, the details of which shall remain secret until they all arrive at the airport.

What starts out as a bit of festive fun transforms into a life-changing experience when excitement, adventure and romance combine for a Christmas the sisters will *never* forget…

Join eldest sister Sienna on her sun-soaked adventures in Bora-Bora in

Mistletoe Magic in Tahiti
by Kandy Shepherd

Travel to the stunning Costa Rican rainforest with youngest sister Eliza in

Cinderella's Costa Rican Adventure
by Scarlet Wilson

Wrap up warm as you head to the mountains of Japan with middle sister Thea in

Snowbound Reunion in Japan
by Nina Milne

Dear Reader,

Christmas is a special time for me, centering around family and close friends. It would be quite a shock if suddenly I was faced with a Christmas Day completely on my own in a foreign country! That's exactly what happens to my heroine, Sienna Kendall, along with her sisters, Thea and Eliza, when they make a pact to do something daringly different for Christmas.

To Sienna's delight, she ends up on the tropical island of Bora-Bora, a Tahitian paradise and one of the most romantic destinations on earth. Still reeling from a nasty divorce, Sienna isn't looking for love, but when she meets gorgeous Kai Hunter, the chemistry between them sizzles. Kai is enchanted by lovely Sienna, but he's facing complex life decisions. There are ups and downs before these two realize they've found not just a holiday romance, but a lifetime love!

Mistletoe Magic in Tahiti is the first book of three in The Christmas Pact series. The next two books tell the stories of Sienna's sisters—*Cinderella's Costa Rican Adventure* by Scarlet Wilson and *Snowbound Reunion in Japan* by Nina Milne. It was such a pleasure to work with two such talented authors on this deeply romantic series!

Warm regards,

Kandy Shepherd

Mistletoe Magic in Tahiti

—

Kandy Shepherd

Special thanks and acknowledgment are given to
Kandy Shepherd for her contribution to
The Christmas Pact miniseries.

Recycling programs
for this product may
not exist in your area.

ISBN-13: 978-1-335-59642-0

Mistletoe Magic in Tahiti

Copyright © 2023 by Harlequin Enterprises ULC

For questions and comments about the quality of this book, please contact us at CustomerService@Harlequin.com.

Harlequin Enterprises ULC
22 Adelaide St. West, 41st Floor
Toronto, Ontario M5H 4E3, Canada
www.Harlequin.com

Printed in U.S.A.

Kandy Shepherd swapped a career as a magazine editor for a life writing romance. She lives on a small farm in the Blue Mountains near Sydney, Australia, with her husband, daughter and lots of pets. She believes in love at first sight and real-life romance—they worked for her! Kandy loves to hear from her readers. Visit her at kandyshepherd.com.

Books by Kandy Shepherd

Harlequin Romance

Christmas at the Harrington Park Hotel

Their Royal Baby Gift

How to Make a Wedding

From Bridal Designer to Bride

Stranded with Her Greek Tycoon
Best Man and the Runaway Bride
Second Chance with the Single Dad
Falling for the Secret Princess
One Night with Her Millionaire Boss
Second Chance with His Cinderella
Pregnancy Shock for the Greek Billionaire

Visit the Author Profile page
at Harlequin.com for more titles.

To two wonderful people, my daughter, Lucy,
for her insights on character and my son-in-law,
Jamie Lee, for his extensive knowledge of surfing
and water sports, which he kindly shared with me
for this story. Thank you!

Praise for
Kandy Shepherd

"*Falling for the Secret Princess* is a sweet and
swoon-worthy romance. Author Kandy Shepherd
wrote this beautiful romance which would take
you far, far away.... As a romance reader this is
the ultimate escape. The storyline had plenty of
twists and turns and would keep you engrossed
till the end. Highly recommended for all readers of
romance."

—*Goodreads*

PROLOGUE

SIENNA KENDALL LOVED Christmas in London—the dazzling store decorations, the festive carols, the spectacular lights on Regents Street, the giant tree in Trafalgar Square, ice-skating in Hyde Park, people scurrying around burdened with parcels wishing random strangers season's greetings. If you were lucky, there was snow. But most of all Sienna loved the celebration with her close-knit family—her parents and younger sisters, Thea and Eliza—at the house in which they'd grown up in the west London suburb of Chiswick.

Year after year Christmas was the same, even after the sisters had left home. The three sisters and their mum and dad cooked together, and after their feast—always turkey with all the trimmings—watched a Christmas film, the more sentimental the better. Boyfriends, and in Sienna's case her now ex-husband, and friends who found themselves alone at Christmas would sometimes join them. But at the core of the celebrations was the family.

They'd start the festivities by trimming the tree together, each of them adding a new ornament for that year. The tree had become delightfully crowded with their contributions, until two years ago a kitten Sienna was fostering had jumped up on the tree and pulled it crashing down, smashing a number of ornaments. Fortunately, they hadn't been special ones and, after an initial shocked gasp, they'd all dissolved into laughter and her mother had proclaimed it a good excuse to stock up on new ornaments at the after-Christmas sales. And wasn't it more important that the kitten was unharmed?

A Kendall Christmas was full of laughter, familiar traditions and rituals and the security of knowing that no matter what else might go wrong in her life, thirty-two-year-old Sienna would always be warmed by the love of her family.

Not so this year. In early October, over Sunday lunch at a favourite Chiswick pub overlooking the Thames, out of the blue her parents announced they were doing something different for Christmas this year.

'We've booked a month-long cruise to the Caribbean over Christmas,' her father said. 'On our own.' He and her mother smiled at each other. It was a smile that gently but firmly excluded their grown-up daughters.

Sienna was too shocked and wounded to say

anything. Her sisters seemed equally flabbergasted. They all just stared at their parents.

Finally, her younger sister Eliza broke the silence. 'Wh-what?'

'Why would you do this?' Sienna managed to get out.

'What the—?' said Thea.

'It's our fortieth anniversary this year. We wanted to do something just for ourselves,' her mother said. 'You have your own lives, your own circle of friends. I thought you might appreciate the chance to do something different this time.'

Sienna was too bewildered to make sense of what her mother was saying. Christmas was for family. Why would her parents change such a long-standing tradition?

She didn't want anything to be different this Christmas.

Then she saw her mum exchange a few quiet words with Eliza and she began to understand. Her sister, seven years younger than she was, had been diagnosed with acute myeloid leukaemia when she was six, and a second time when she was fourteen. She had also been unwell on occasions in between. Over those years, the family had all pulled together to look after her, her mother stepping down from her career as a schoolteacher. One reason it was so important to make Christmas special each year was to celebrate that Eliza was still with them.

Now Eliza had been completely discharged from hospital with no more follow-ups. The care by her parents over those years must have been an enormous pressure, even if everything they'd done had been done out of love. No wonder they wanted a complete break, just the two of them.

'Of course, I understand,' Sienna said.

That she'd guessed right was confirmed by Eliza, her voice a little shaky as she addressed their parents. 'You'll have a fantastic time, all that sightseeing, with someone making every single meal for you. You deserve it, both of you.'

'Absolutely, you must go,' said Thea.

In a world turned upside down by divorce, Sienna wanted, *needed*, this part of her life to stay the same. Of course her parents deserved their dream cruise, but Christmas simply wouldn't be the same without them. For the first time there would be just the three girls on Christmas Day—and it would seem weird.

Turned out that wasn't to be, either.

Eliza beckoned to them. 'Sienna, Thea, come and help me get another round of drinks.'

Once the sisters were out of their parents' sight, Eliza pulled them down onto some chairs at another table.

Sienna could tell her little sister was shaken

by their parents' change of plan for Christmas. 'You okay?'

She reached out to cover her hand with hers and Thea did the same. Protecting her, as they had always done. Although Eliza was well now, Sienna found it hard to step down from her role as fiercely protective big sister.

'We have to let them go. They've spent years worrying about me,' said Eliza. 'You all have. They need a chance to concentrate on themselves again.'

Sienna sighed. 'Agreed. But is it wrong that I'm an adult yet still love coming to our parents' house for Christmas to spend time with my family?'

'Me too,' said Thea.

'We all do,' said Eliza. 'But this year, it has to be different.'

Thea gave a small groan. 'What will we do instead?'

'We do something different, too,' said Eliza. 'A Christmas adventure of our own. I think we should step outside our comfort zones and each go away for Christmas.'

'By ourselves?' Sienna choked out. 'Even you?'

'Yes, even you, Eliza?' Thea asked, obviously as disconcerted as Sienna.

'Especially me,' Eliza said with a stubborn tilt to her chin Sienna didn't recognise. 'Let's make a pact.'

Sienna's brow furrowed. 'A pact? We haven't done that since we were kids.'

'This will be our Christmas pact—to each go away for two weeks over Christmas,' said Eliza. 'We will choose a place for each other to go and do it in secret. Each destination will be a complete surprise. We pack each other's cases, and only find out our destinations when we arrive at the airport.'

Eliza sounded very sure of her plan, although Sienna suspected her sister was making it up as she went along.

'She's lost it,' said Thea, shaking her head and smiling at Sienna.

'She has,' agreed Sienna. 'But it's not the worst idea I've heard.'

What was the alternative? The depressing prospect of Christmas in the house without their parents? Kicking around with friends who all had their own families to go home to for Christmas? Why not take the opportunity to do something daringly different—a vacation each on their own?

'I like that we will challenge ourselves,' Sienna said.

'I like that we get to pick for each other,' said Thea.

'We're really going to do this?' asked Eliza. 'It could be brilliant.'

Sienna nodded. 'We're doing it,' she said confidently. 'Right, Thea?'

Thea nodded too, and laughed. 'What have I just let myself in for?'

Sienna held out one fist, her knuckles facing her sisters. 'To the Christmas pact.'

'To the Christmas pact!' Thea and Eliza replied, bumping their fists against Sienna's.

CHAPTER ONE

Every time Sienna Kendall heard the French Polynesian island of Bora Bora described as paradise, she wholeheartedly agreed. Dressed in a bikini, reclining on a lounger on a beach renowned to be one of the best in the world, a chilled tropical fruit cocktail to hand, she thought Bora Bora checked every possible paradise box. Glorious, clear aquamarine waters with the majestic Mount Otemanu in the background. Sugar-white sands. Sun. Palm trees everywhere she looked. Blue skies dotted with the multicoloured sails of kitesurfers. All overlaid with the utmost in French luxury and style.

Her sisters, Thea and Eliza, could not have chosen a more perfect destination for Sienna's first ever Christmas away from home when they'd booked this trip as her surprise location. On many a gloomy winter day in London she had fantasised about escaping to a Tahitian island like Bora Bora. It was perfect.

Yet, since she'd been here, she had never felt more alone. Her sisters had overlooked one important detail about Bora Bora—it was above all a paradise for couples, a dream destination for honeymooners. Aged thirty-two and shakily single after the nastiest of nasty divorces, Sienna was surrounded by canoodling couples. Everything in her fabulous overwater villa was set up for two, from the toiletries to the 'his and hers' lush velvet bathrobes. Last night the enormous bed had been turned down on one lonely side for just her, the single occupant of a definitely double room.

Her aloneness was magnified by the prospect in ten days of her very first Christmas without her sisters and parents: *Would she be all by herself on Christmas Day?*

She shuddered at the thought. But her sisters would be facing the same.

The Christmas pact did, in retrospect, seem a crazy plan. But wasn't booking each sister into an unknown destination an adventure— and certainly a challenge? She and Thea had booked Eliza into a treetop resort in the Costa Rican rainforest; then, together with Eliza, she'd organised a trip for Thea to the winter wonderland of a top Japanese ski resort.

When Sienna had rocked up to Heathrow Airport on the fourteenth of December, her eyes had misted with tears of gratitude and love when she'd discovered her surprise destination was Bora Bora. Thea and Eliza knew her so well. Her ex-husband Callum was a skier and for so many of the years they'd been together, her vacations had been in the snow while she'd longed to escape the British winter to a tropical island. Bora Bora was truly a wonderful choice. She hoped her sisters had been as surprised and delighted by her choices for them.

She was determined to enjoy every minute of her stay here. This morning, her second day on the island, she had escaped the solitude of her luxurious villa and made her way to the postcard-beautiful beach where there were more people. The inevitable loved-up couples, yes, but also teenagers, children and a doting pair of grandparents lavishing attention on an adorable baby girl dressed in a ruffled pink swimsuit. Sienna had to avert her eyes from the toddler and look back at her mystery novel although she didn't see the words as more than a blur on the page. She had always wanted children and had mistakenly thought her ex-husband had too. It was a pain that wasn't easy to heal, nor were the bitter thoughts berating her for being such a fool as to stay in that dead-in-the-water marriage for ten years.

Peals of girlish laughter made her look up

from her unread book. The laughter came from two young teenage girls on kite boards who flew by quite close to shore. They were attached by harnesses to kites that billowed above them as each girl steered with a control bar she held in front of her. Sienna was struck at how happy and carefree the young people looked. How long since she had felt such unbridled joy? She swallowed hard against a sudden lump of misery.

She couldn't *remember*.

Zooming along on the water like that must give such an adrenaline buzz. Perhaps she should try it while she was on the island. To challenge herself was part of the Christmas pact.

The girls were with a guy in his thirties who appeared to be their instructor. He too was laughing, as he called encouraging comments in French and skilfully manoeuvred his board close enough to help, far away enough not to impede.

As he came more into Sienna's sight, she caught her breath. He was hot. Really hot. So hot she couldn't stop staring at him. Tall, strong, with muscles defined by a short-sleeved black wetsuit, dark hair wet against his head, smooth brown skin, a smile that showed perfect white teeth and that made her want to smile back, even though he wasn't looking anywhere near her.

She slipped on her dark sunglasses as she

watched him—watched *them*. She was watching the girls too, not just their handsome instructor; of course she was. All three skilfully rode their boards to the farther end of the beach, then pulled the boards high onto the sand. Must be the end of the lesson. The older couple with the baby girl walked across to meet the instructor. Sienna watched as he swung the baby up into his arms and gave her a big smack of a kiss on each cheek as she laughed and squealed in delight. The sight of this big, strong man with the tiny toddler wrenched at her heart, it was so beautiful. He was obviously close to her. Was he her father? The cruellest thing Callum had done in a litany of cruelties was to tell her he didn't want children, and if she wanted a baby she'd better go and find another husband to give her one. Finding another husband was the last thing she, with her bruised and shattered heart, wanted. Ever.

The older couple left with the girls after hugs all round. Did she dare walk up to the instructor and ask him if he could teach her to kitesurf? She couldn't see a logo of a school on either the boards or the kites. If she wanted to learn from him, she'd have to approach him herself.

Just do it.

After all, wasn't that what this vacation in Bora Bora was all about—taking new risks, doing different things she mightn't have dared to do before? Kitesurfing could be one of those things. So could finding the courage to stroll right up to this gorgeous man and introduce herself.

The closer she got to him, the better he looked. That black wetsuit moulded every muscle, and the short sleeves didn't quite cover some interesting looking Tahitian tattoos. By the time she faced him, she was a stuttering wreck.

He didn't notice she was there. She cleared her throat and he looked up from where he was detaching the harness from the board. 'Um… I…I wonder could I…I book a lesson with you? Kitesurfing looks such fun and I'd really like to try it.'

He stood up to his full height and again Sienna had to catch her breath. She was tall, but he was taller and she had never seen a more magnificent looking man in her life. Please let him say *yes*.

Kai Hunter was so taken aback by the request from the beautiful brown-haired woman in the bronze bikini, it took him a moment to gather his thoughts. Did she really believe he was a kitesurfing instructor? If people here didn't recognise him as the public face of his company Wave Hunters, a leading brand in water sports equipment, they would certainly know him as the international surfing champion who, when he was younger, had represented Tahiti in many surfing competitions around the world. Then there were the people who knew him because of his family, wealthy and well connected. He'd been notorious as the black sheep—*le mauvais élève*—of that family.

But she was a tourist. English by the sound of her accent. Why would she have any idea who he was? It was an honest mistake. He should refer her straightaway to the excellent instructors at the kitesurfing school on the island. But before he could say something, she spoke again.

'The girls you were teaching looked so happy,' she said, a note of wistfulness in her voice. 'They seemed to get more skilful by the minute.'

'They're good,' he said.

That was because they were his nieces and were helping him test a new style of harness he was developing for Wave Hunters' kitesurfing equipment division.

'You're obviously a good teacher.'

He shrugged, not wanting to go there.

'Is kitesurfing very difficult?' she asked with a slight frown.

'Not as difficult as it might look.'

'That's reassuring.'

'You've never tried it?'

He couldn't help but be intrigued. She was as elegant as a woman could look wearing just a bikini, her shoulder-length hair stylishly cut and streaked, a thick gold chain around her neck, smart leather sandals. This kind of tourist often wanted to do nothing livelier than lie on the beach topping up their tans with an occasional splash in the water to cool off. Kitesurfing took energy, strength and commitment.

'Never,' she said.

'What about surfing?'

He was acting like an instructor sounding out her water sports skill levels. Which wasn't at all the way he wanted this conversation to go. Yet there was something about the longing in her voice that made him reluctant to give her an out-and-out *no*.

'Never. Although I'd like to try that too.'

Not on Bora Bora she wouldn't. Only the most experienced surfed at Teavanui Pass where the waves broke over treacherous coral reefs. It was definitely not for beginners.

Again, before he could say anything, she continued. 'But I'm good at snowboarding, and watching you and the girls, I think that skill could come in useful.'

'Yes, it would. But—'

I'm not an instructor, he tried to say.

'That's a relief,' she said. 'Because I really want

to try this. And I'd be so grateful if you could help me.'

She took off her dark sunglasses and looked up at him. Her eyes were a pure, cool green that mesmerised him. 'Before you ask, I'm a competent swimmer. I dare say I'll fall in more than once as I get the hang of it.' Her lips curved into a smile, self-deprecating but with an intriguing hint of mischief. She flexed her right arm. 'And I'm strong. See, muscles. Lots of time spent at the gym in London.'

Did she sense, somehow, his reluctance as an instructor? That she had to sell herself as a suitable potential student? If so, it was working. Would it hurt him to give her a lesson? His business took him around the world. Last week he'd been in Sydney, Australia, the week before that in San Francisco and Hawaii, with future visits planned to Sri Lanka and Vietnam. But he always came home for Christmas and he didn't have anything planned for the rest of the day.

'I've got time for one lesson after lunch,' he said.

'Perfect,' she said with that smile he found so appealing.

'Say, two o'clock. Here.'

'What do I need to bring with me for the lesson?'

'Just yourself,' he said.

Through narrowed eyes, he sized her up for a wetsuit. She was tall and slender with—as she'd boasted—gym-toned arms and legs. Perhaps his gaze lingered a tad too long on her breasts and gently flaring hips.

He caught her eye and realised she was aware of his appraisal of her body. To deny it would be futile. She held his gaze, her eyes lit by the warmth of that smile. He saw that she was amused, and that she was doing some appraisal of her own and not finding him wanting.

'Meet back here at two,' he said gruffly.

'Thank you!' she said, beaming.

For a moment Kai thought she was going to throw her arms around him.

For a disconcerting moment he wished she would.

CHAPTER TWO

WAS IT JET LAG sending Sienna's thoughts into a spin? After all, it had been a long flight from London, changing planes in Los Angeles to fly to the Tahitian capital of Papeete, then a small plane onto the airport on the island of Motu Mute, followed by a boat transfer to her resort on the actual island of Bora Bora. There was a ten-hour time difference between London and Bora Bora, which she found a tad confusing.

Not jet lag, she thought.

More like she was in a tizz at the prospect of her kitesurfing lesson. Or—if she dug deeper—was it the handsome kitesurfing instructor? Whatever the irrational excitement was, it had sent her, once back in her suite, into a frenzy of exfoliation, depilation, moisturising and the careful application of toenail polish.

Now she twisted and turned in front of the hotel mirror to critically examine how she looked in her favourite sleek, black one-piece swimsuit that thankfully her sisters had packed for her. A swimsuit she wore for swimming laps, more appropriate for kitesurfing than the sexy bronze bikini she'd worn to the beach this morning. When she'd arrived in Bora Bora and unpacked, she'd found the gift-wrapped bikini in her suitcase, with a card saying:

Open now. Don't wait for Christmas Day! Love from Thea

The bikini bore an exclusive Italian label and must have cost Thea a bomb, but that was her generous sister all over. Sienna loved her gift. Not just because it was a designer bikini, but also because of the thought behind it. Thea knew how Sienna's ex-husband, Callum's, behaviour had eroded her confidence as a woman. She hoped Thea would appreciate as much the thermal socks she and Eliza had packed in their sister's bag.

As she headed to the designated spot for her kitesurfing lesson, Sienna realised she had no idea of her instructor's name. She'd been so delighted that he'd agreed to teach her, she hadn't given it a thought. What if he wasn't there? She didn't know what kitesurfing school he was affiliated with to get in touch. She realised how deeply disappointed she'd be if he wasn't there.

This feeling wasn't something she could explain. She didn't know anything about the guy except he had a great body and an amazing smile. And that he might be the father of a baby girl. Which meant he might be married to the mother of that baby girl.

But why did that even matter? She wasn't looking for a date. Just the chance to try a new sport and take a further step away from a life that had been shaped more by the needs and desires of her ex-husband than by her own. If the teacher just happened to be a gorgeous man, then all the better. She'd sensed he had found her attractive too and that had made her feel good—thank you, bronze bikini. He was probably a flirt—just like many of the snowboarding and ski instructors she'd met over the years of Callum-led ski resort vacations—so she certainly wouldn't take his admiration seriously, but she'd take it all the same.

Her fears that he wouldn't show up were groundless. She was a carefully timed five minutes early—ten minutes would appear too keen, whereas to aim for on-time risked her being late. But there he was, a little farther down the beach, near the shade of a group of palm trees. There was no one else with him. How many others in the class? She hadn't thought to ask that, either.

He stood facing out to the water and she

couldn't help pausing to admire his back view: broad shoulders, tight butt, long, strong legs defined by the black wetsuit.

You did not find men like this in London.

She had to clear her throat to speak and he turned to face her.

She swallowed a gasp. He was every bit as hot as she'd remembered—more so, perhaps, with his black hair dried to a wavy mass to his shoulders. His expression was still and serious, as if she'd caught him in the middle of some important thought that had taken him far away from this beach. Their gazes connected, his eyes a warm, compelling brown.

For a long moment all she was aware of was him, his strength, his power, the way he seemed part of the landscape as much as that glorious aquamarine water of the lagoon sparkling in the sunshine, the palm leaves that rustled in the breeze. The air between them seemed to shimmer as if something invisible connected them. Her heart started to thud.

Then two young boys shouting to each other ran by on the beach behind him, and the moment was shattered.

He walked towards her with the welcoming smile of an instructor awaiting his client, that faraway look banished to be replaced by polite greeting. Sienna shook her head to clear it of all sorts of fanciful thoughts. She really must have jet lag. That moment of such intense awareness had felt like some kind of hallucination.

He nodded in acknowledgment of her presence. 'Right on time,' he said.

'I…I'm sorry, I didn't tell you my name,' she stuttered. 'You…you might have needed it to book the lesson. I'm Sienna Kendall.'

'I didn't tell you mine, either,' he said with a slow grin as he looked down into her face. Her heart fluttered. It seriously did. 'Kai Hunter.'

Kai Hunter.

Even his name was gorgeous.

And that French accent.

He really was too good to be true. Was it shallow of her to delight in how good-looking he was? Maybe that was what that strange moment had been about, her senses overwhelmed by his good looks.

She would love to take a selfie alongside Kai to send to her sisters. She'd add a smirk emoji to her boast: *My kitesurfing instructor—just sayin'*…

Did some small, damaged part of her wish Callum could see her with a man like Kai Hunter? The answer to that was a resounding no. Any love, any attraction, she'd once felt for her ex-husband had boiled down to an absolute indifference. She didn't want him to know anything she was doing—despite the satisfaction it might give her.

But no photos from Bora Bora would go on social media. She'd left her phone behind in the hotel room. As an interior designer, she had built up an enormous following when she'd started posting her design projects online, usually several times a day. She actually had the title of a design 'influencer' now. However, she had promised her sisters—and herself—that she would put work aside and take this time to rest, recuperate and place the hideousness of the divorce behind her.

Please put yourself first for a change, Eliza had urged. *And don't even think about work.*

Sienna had agreed, although with secret reluctance. She'd spent years building up her design business; she dreaded it might be harmed by a two-week break from social media. These days she actually earned more from product endorsements than she did from design fees.

She forced her voice to a neutral friendliness, unaffected by his proximity. 'Hi Kai, good to see you again.' She looked around. 'How many others are in the class? Are they late?'

'No others. It's just you.'

'Just me?' The words came out as a decidedly uncool squeak. She forced her voice to sound more normal. 'You mean it's a private lesson?'

'One-on-one is the most effective way to learn to kitesurf.' His voice was pleasing, deep and husky.

One-on-one with Kai Hunter sounded good to her.

'Just clarifying,' she said, feeling a little light-headed.

'You okay with that?'

'Of course,' she said, supressing a little shudder of excitement. 'I'm sure I'll learn faster that way and I really want to kitesurf.'

Eliza had said her Christmas gift to her would be a group water sports lesson, but a private lesson would cost more. She would text Eliza to say she would pay any difference in cost. Her baby sister's education and work experience had been interrupted by her episodes of illness, and she didn't yet have the same earning power as she and Thea, who was a corporate lawyer. She and Thea had insisted on going halves in paying for Eliza's Costa Rican stay. A minor squabble had erupted over Eliza's protests that she could pay for herself, thank you very much, and to stop mothering—only she'd called it *smothering*—her. She and Thea had won.

'Do you have two hours?' Kai asked.

'Absolutely.' She looked longingly to the tantalising blue waters of the lagoon. 'I can't wait to be flying along over there.'

He smiled. 'I like your enthusiasm. But you need to be familiar with operating the kite before you get in the water. Safety is priority. You'll be staying on the sand for the first part of the lesson.'

She frowned. 'On the sand? How does that work?'

'You'll learn how to operate the kite by piloting it as you walk along the beach. I will be with you all the time, showing you what to do.'

'That's reassuring.'

'It's my job as a kitesurfing instructor,' he said. She wondered why that seemed funny to him as he obviously fought to suppress laughter. 'Let's get started,' he said.

'Makes sense,' she said. 'I guess I'll have to be patient.'

He led her over to where a board and sail lay, weighted down with sand to keep it still in the breeze. He handed her a lightweight wetsuit with short sleeves and legs, branded with a colourful Wave Hunters logo. 'You'll need this before we get a harness onto you,' he said. 'The harness can chafe bare skin, and the wetsuit gives sun protection as well.'

Wave Hunters. She'd seen that brand on swimwear; it was well known in water sports. The wetsuit was new, she noted approvingly; she had to tear a tag off it. She started to put it on, but she had never worn a wetsuit before. It was surprisingly tight and she had to wiggle to get into it.

'Want help?' Kai asked as she fumbled for the zipper that ran down her back.

He was respectful. Didn't make any move to touch her without permission. But Sienna's immediate reaction was to flinch and step back from him so quickly she nearly tripped over herself.

'I'm fine, thank you,' she said hastily—too hastily. And immediately wished she hadn't acted like such an adolescent. She hoped he didn't take offence. It wasn't that she didn't trust him. Certainly not that she didn't like him. But because she didn't trust herself.

Her marriage to Callum had been floundering for several years before she'd finally caught him cheating—as in blatantly having sex in their marital bed, in their house, with a woman from his gym. That time he couldn't deny it, as he'd denied it so many times before. Over the years, he'd gaslighted her, making her believe she was imagining the signs of his infidelities, that she was too suspicious, neurotic, a nag. His worst accusation had been that she didn't trust him— the lying, cheating man who was supposed to love her. Her distrust had very good cause, as it turned out. Over the years with Callum, she'd got used to hiding her true feelings until it had become second nature.

Now, on the surface, she was ready and eager to start her lesson. But running under that surface was a super-charged awareness of magnificent Kai Hunter. She hadn't been this close to a man she found attractive, who wasn't her husband, for so many years she couldn't remember. She'd met Callum on their first week at university, married him at age twenty-three, and there hadn't been anyone else since. She was a thirty-two-year-old woman with the dating experience of a teenager.

Not that this was a date. Of course it wasn't; she had to keep reminding herself of that. But it was just him and her—*one-on-one*—and she simply wasn't used to it. She was way too aware of the sheer maleness of him, as if every nerve in her body was on alert. And she couldn't let him guess how on edge that made her feel. A man like this would most likely have women flinging themselves at him all the time. She didn't want him to think she was one of them.

She managed to slide up the zipper without any help.

'Let's get started,' Kai said. If he'd noticed her flinch away from him, he certainly didn't show it. 'Before we get you into the harness that will attach you to the kite, I'll explain the basics.'

The basics had to do mainly with wind direction. He explained she needed to have an onshore wind at her back, how the wind would propel the kite above her and how she would have to pilot it using the control bar that was attached by strings to the canopy. She got it, sort of, but her confusion showed.

'You'll understand it better once you try it,' he said. 'That's the best way to learn.'

She stood very still as he helped her into the harness, which wrapped around her hips. His hands were sure and deft. She held her breath. This touch was purely professional and necessary but she was hyper-sensitively aware of it. Once in the harness, he attached the kite to the harness.

'I'm sorry, I'm not used to this,' she said, apologising for her awkwardness.

'Of course you're not. It's your first time kite-surfing,' he said easily.

But she didn't mean that. She meant being in such close proximity to a man she found so compellingly attract she was not sure how to handle it.

'Okay?'

'Raring to go.'

Straightaway the kite lifted with the light

wind. 'Wow! I'm really feeling it,' she said, on a surge of excitement.

'Conditions are good for a beginner,' Kai said. 'We're lucky. We're coming into our wet season but there are no signs of rain today.'

He showed her how to manoeuvre the canopy with the control bar, to vary the power and the speed to keep it in the safe power zone. She walked slowly up the beach as she followed his instructions. 'Is this right?'

'You're doing great.'

Kai was an excellent teacher, patient and funny and kind. Her confidence grew.

She could do this.

Her last instruction on the sand was to practice sitting down on the sand and letting the kite pull her to her feet. 'Are you ready to get in the water? Because I think you are,' he said.

'Yes!' she said.

'You'll stay in waist-deep water and I'll always be close by. I'm here to keep you safe.'

He was strong, protective and she did indeed feel safe with him. 'Thank you.' Her eyes met his and this time there was nothing magical there, just reassurance and kindness that, after living with a man who had let her down so badly, was a kind of magic of its own.

Her first water start was a success as, sitting in the water, she slipped her feet into the loops on the board, and let the kite pull her up so she was standing upright. Kai was alongside in the water reminding her of how to use the bar.

She exulted in the feeling as she flew across the water, in harmony with the wind. This was amazing, even beyond expectations. 'I'm off! I'm kitesurfing!'

Beginner's luck. It wasn't long before the kite fell and she splashed backwards into the water. But she persevered and by the end of the lesson she felt she had the hang of kitesurfing as a beginner. 'I'm loving this, Kai. It's the best fun ever!' she called as she flew past him, the canopy high above her.

He laughed and called more encouragement. She realised she had lost all self-consciousness around him.

Kai had never seen anyone get so far so fast at their first attempt at kitesurfing. He was impressed. Seriously impressed. Sienna was super fit, smart, took directions and learned quickly. She had a natural aptitude for the sport, was probably very good at snowboarding and would most likely make a good surfer.

But it was more than that. More than her being beautiful. He liked her. Really liked her. He'd felt totally at ease with her from the get-go. She was open. Friendly. The first to laugh and make fun of her mistakes in that self-effacing way British people sometimes did.

Kai wasn't a kitesurfing teacher. Not a paid one. Never had been. Although he had taught surfing as one of his part-time jobs when he was younger. When he'd had to leave home to escape the disapproval of his parents and what his high-achieving family considered to be his failure.

His father was a top lawyer in Papeete; his mother held an important government position. His two older brothers had done exactly what had been expected of them; one was a lawyer, the other a doctor. They'd both excelled at private school in Papeete, gone on to university in France. While Kai had dropped out before the final high school exams and gone surfing.

He'd surfed all around the world, collecting titles and big prize money. It hadn't impressed his parents. That kind of success simply hadn't counted in their conservative world. But his grandparents had believed in him. They'd given him a home on their private island off Bora Bora where they lived, and a series of jobs in the resort they owned on Bora Bora. And then given him the seed money he'd needed to start his own business—a loan he'd insisted on repaying years ago. His parents hadn't stopped caring about him on some level, he had to believe that, but only when they couldn't deny the financial success of Wave Hunters had they come to respect him. Success in business counted in their world and he'd found success in spades. Still, the relationship with his parents remained uneasy.

He was glad he'd gone along, on impulse, with Sienna's assumption he was an instructor. Otherwise, he would have missed the opportunity to meet this delightful woman. He wanted to see her again and was pleased when, at the end of the lesson, she asked if she could book a lesson with him the next day.

'I've only scratched the surface of kitesurfing, haven't I?' she said once they were back on the sand. She was flushed with exertion, those awesome green eyes bright with exhilaration. 'I want to learn to jump and turn and do fun things like I saw you do this morning.'

'That might take longer than two lessons.' He didn't want to dampen her enthusiasm, and she was obviously an athlete, but those skills took time.

'I've got the time. I'm here for another ten days. So you're okay for another lesson? Same time tomorrow?'

'Sure.' The charade couldn't go on longer than that, though. It would take just one comment from a friend on the beach to blow his cover. And that would be awkward for both Sienna and for him.

'Another private lesson?' she said. 'I really feel I learned faster one-on-one.'

He nodded in agreement. 'It's the most efficient way to learn.'

He would like to ask her to meet him for a drink, to talk to her about more than kitesurfing. In other words, a date. But he knew nothing about her. Sienna didn't wear a ring but that didn't signify anything. He had to be sure of her status. Married women were completely out of bounds. And it was surprising the number of married women on vacation looking for a fling, even when they were staying in the same room with their husbands. He'd been burned by one such woman back when he'd been a naive teenager. Sienna hadn't mentioned a partner, but there hadn't been much opportunity for chitchat; it had been a full-on lesson, accelerated when he'd realised how quickly she was picking up skills.

'Are you here with someone?' he asked.

Her chin rose, defensively, he thought. 'No. I'm here on my own.'

'By yourself on a honeymoon island?'

She rolled her eyes. 'Yes, I didn't realise it would be quite so full of couples. Neither did my sister.'

He must have misunderstood her. 'You're here with your sister?'

She wrinkled her nose in a gesture he found cute. 'That didn't come out right, did it? I'm not here with my sister. Either of my two sisters, actually. One's in Costa Rica and the other is in Japan.'

'They live there?'

'No, we all live in London.' She paused, a smile hovering around her mouth. 'I'm not explaining this very well, am I? My sisters and I made a pact to each do something exciting and different for Christmas this year. On our own.'

'Like kitesurfing in Bora Bora?'

'Exactly. And skiing in Japan for one sister, with a visit to an eco-resort in Costa Rica for the other. I believe zip lining is on the agenda for her. But our destinations weren't known to us until we were actually at the airport, as each of our trips had been booked as a surprise.'

There was a story behind that unusual arrangement. Why did these sisters need to challenge themselves? Why was this beautiful woman on her own? Were the men in London blind?

'And you're happy they chose Bora Bora for you?' he said.

She gracefully waved her arm to indicate their surroundings. 'Of course. This truly is a paradise.

I love it. I wouldn't want to be anywhere else. Especially after our lesson today.'

Her enthusiasm was one of the things he found so appealing about her. In repose her face was quite serious, intent and very attractive. But when she was smiling and animated, he could not keep his eyes off her.

'That's an unusual way to book a vacation,' he said.

'It is, isn't it?' she said. 'We'll laugh about it one day, I suppose. But my sisters made an excellent choice for me.'

Kai thought so too. He wanted to know more about Sienna Kendall.

'You're not here on your honeymoon, or with your sister...but do you have a man in your life?'

'Heavens no. I...I'm recently divorced.'

That explained a lot. The skittishness when he got close. The way her eyes fluttered before they met his.

'I'm sorry,' he said.

He was pleased.

'Don't be. I'm very happy to be divorced. It... It wasn't a good marriage.' But it was hurt rather than happiness that momentarily clouded her eyes. Kai might have to tread carefully here. But that wouldn't stop him from getting to know the delightful Sienna Kendall.

'And you? Are you married, I mean,' she said.

'Never come close to it,' he said.

Their eyes met and it was like that strange sensation he'd felt earlier when he'd been caught in her gaze. Long ago he'd learned to trust his instincts; they'd always steered him in the right direction. Right now, somewhere deep in his gut, was a feeling this woman—impossible as it might seem—could be someone memorable and important in his life.

Sienna fumbled with the back zipper of her wetsuit. She looked back over her shoulder at him. 'I…er…might need some help here with the zipper to get out of this.'

Was he reading an invitation in her narrowed eyes? He was way too aware of her—not as a kitesurfing student but as a highly desirable woman—to offer to help in case he'd got her completely wrong. He could imagine only too well what it would be like to unpeel her from the wetsuit to reveal that sleek black swimsuit she wore underneath. Wet, it would highlight every enticing curve. Curves he would like to caress and explore.

He cleared his throat, but even so his voice came out husky. 'It's okay. Wear it back to your resort. You'll need it for tomorrow's lesson.'

He didn't want to get in too deep with her. Yet.

CHAPTER THREE

SIENNA WAS THRILLED when lesson two the next day went even better than the first. After a few more supervised rides, she felt confident enough to take off on her own. Kai rode alongside on his own board while keeping a careful eye on her. The inevitable mishaps weren't serious, and she laughed as she got herself up and skimming along on the water again. All those hours in the gym had paid off in strength and resilience. She'd worked out not so much in pursuit of a perfect body, but to physically power through the pain of the loss of her marriage. As well, it had been something to do in the lonely hours of the evening when she simply couldn't face the suddenly empty house. She hadn't had to live on her own for long in the beautiful home she had remodelled and decorated but had been defiled by her ex and that woman. It had been put on the market and she and her cat had moved back to her parents' home in Chiswick. But the gym habit had stayed.

'Are you sure you haven't done this before?' Kai called across to her after she successfully attempted a small jump.

'I swear I haven't, but I wish I had,' she said breathlessly. 'I'm loving it.'

She'd been visiting friends in Cornwall when she'd first noticed kitesurfers and fancied she'd like to try the sport. And now she'd got the chance—doing something she wanted, when she wanted, without having to prioritise Callum's interests over her own.

The lesson was over all too soon. This time Kai showed her what to do with the kite and harness at the end of a session. As she carefully followed instructions, she had an uneasy feeling there was a sense of finality about what he was doing. That didn't stop her from asking could she book a third lesson for the following day.

Kai stopped what he was doing but stayed crouched on the sand near the board. He looked up to her. 'A third lesson would be useful for you. But I'm not sure I'm the best person to be taking you for that lesson.'

'Oh,' she said, feeling as deflated as the kite lying slack on the sand. 'I see.' So she wouldn't see him again? She was surprised at how much that hurt. She couldn't face his gaze. 'I…I guess you'd prefer to teach more experienced people than me.'

'It's not that at all.' He uncurled that magnificent body to stand up and look down to face her. Tall, imposing, *hot.* 'It's been a privilege to start you on your way. You're good. You could be really good.'

'Then… Then why—?'

He looked very serious. 'It's not something I can explain here.'

'Oh,' she said again, puzzled about what could possibly stop him from continuing to teach her kitesurfing that needed a secret explanation.

'Can you meet me for a drink this evening? We could talk then.'

A rush of relief and elation flooded through her and made her feel light-headed. 'I'd love to have a drink with you. I…I'm intrigued.'

He named a bar at the other end of the beach. 'Can you meet me at six?'

'Yes,' she said, immediately. Did she have to appear so embarrassingly keen? 'I mean, I think I could do that.'

'That's settled, then,' he said. Was that a flicker of relief in his eyes? Was he perhaps expecting her to say no? She couldn't imagine many women would say no to Kai Hunter.

'One thing, though… Actually, two things,' she said. 'First, the wetsuit.' She ran her hands down her sides. 'I love it. It's a perfect fit and so comfortable. I'd like to buy it, please, if that's possible. Then second, paying for my lessons. How do I do that? I'm staying at the Mareva resort. Can I pay at the desk or—?'

'We can sort that out later,' he said with a dismissive wave.

'The wetsuit, too?'

He smiled. 'You really like that wetsuit, don't you?'

'I do. I think it might be a good luck wetsuit. I'm not sure I'd kite surf as well in a different one.'

'A good luck wetsuit? Interesting thought. Some sportspeople have a good luck shirt or a hat or something that gives them confidence. Why not a good luck wetsuit?'

'Why not indeed?' She smiled, knowing he was humouring her but not minding at all.

'I'll see what I can do.'

'It can be my Christmas present to myself,' she said, pleased.

'Do you do that? Buy yourself Christmas presents?'

She nodded. 'That way I get exactly what I want. For birthdays too. Although I don't bother with the gift wrap.'

When Callum had completely forgotten her birthday for the second year in a row, she'd suspected their marriage was past redemption.

When she'd found herself not caring he'd forgotten, she'd known it was completely over.

'Takes all the surprise out of it, though, doesn't it?' Kai said.

'You like surprises?'

'Yes. And when it comes to Christmas presents, I want my presents wrapped up so no matter how much I try to guess what it is, I don't know what my gift is until I unwrap it.'

She laughed. 'I feel the same way about gifts other people give me. So do the rest of my family. We all go to great lengths to disguise our presents so you can't tell what they are until they're opened. One year my sister Eliza gave me a pair of earrings wrapped in a box designed to fit a vacuum cleaner. Christmas is a big deal in our family.'

'Yet you and your sisters have gone away to be on your own for Christmas Day?'

She sobered. 'Yes. Funny that, isn't it? But it's a challenge we all accepted.'

She wasn't comfortable with the way the conversation was going and where it might lead. No way did she want to share the fact she dreaded being on her own on Christmas Day—not with Kai, not with her sisters, not with her parents. The resort where she was staying had signs up promoting their Christmas celebrations; surely there would be fellow guests there who would be friendly once they found she was on her own? Or not. A solitary day in her beautiful over-the-water villa wouldn't be the worst Christmas Day option either. She had to keep telling herself that.

She glanced down at her waterproof watch that tracked steps and other activities and had been an expensive post-divorce present to herself. 'I should be getting back to my resort. Is there anything you need me to help with here before I go?'

'All good here,' he said. 'I'll see you at six.'

As Sienna headed back to the resort, she ran a mental inventory of the clothes her sisters had packed that might be suitable to wear for a drink with a gorgeous guy. She also found herself wondering who Kai would spend Christmas Day with, who chose his gifts and wrapped them in anticipation of his surprise and pleasure, and just what it was he wanted to explain to her.

At the beachside bar, seated at an outside table, Kai watched as Sienna made her way along the sand. She seemed somewhat hesitant, uncertain perhaps about being on her own, and he wondered how long it had been since her divorce.

As she got closer, he caught his breath at how lovely she looked dressed in a simple white sundress that flowed to her ankles, a thigh-high slit revealing glimpses of her long, slim legs as she walked. She smiled as she caught sight of him and put up her hand in a wave. He waved back. He felt an inexplicable surge of pride that of all the guys in the bar giving her the eye, she was there to meet him.

He got up to greet her from the table overlooking the lagoon where he had staked a claim. It would give them a good view as the sun set behind Mount Otemanu; to his eyes there were few sights in the world more splendid. He had to stop himself from greeting Sienna with a kiss on each cheek in the French way—*la bise*. For all the time they'd spent together over the past two days, it had been purely as teacher and student. He sensed he needed to take very slow steps with Sienna when it came to touch.

He'd thought she looked beautiful in a wetsuit, her hair wet, no makeup, smears of sunblock across her face, cheeks flushed in exhilaration. Now she looked elegant, sophisticated, someone who could fit in anywhere. Her hair swung sleek to her shoulders; her green eyes were defined with smoky shadow, her full, kissable mouth slicked with pink lipstick. She wore her gold necklace and an armful of shiny bangles on her right arm. Again, he had to wonder what a woman like this was doing by herself on an island half a world from her home—especially at Christmas.

He settled her at the table and ordered drinks— a beer for him and a fruity yet potent cocktail for her. He clinked his glass to hers. '*Manuia*... cheers.'

'Cheers,' she said. 'What did you say first? How did it go?'

'*Mah-new-yah*. It's the way we say cheers.'

She raised her glass to his again. '*Mah-new-yah,*' she said, in a credible attempt at the Tahitian *te roa* language. It pleased him that she tried.

'What a marvellous place,' she said as she looked around her.

'This bar is very popular, known for its cocktails, and the food is good,' he said.

It was a spacious bar built in a traditional Polynesian style of wooden supports and a roof made of woven pandanus leaf thatch. There was a Christmas tree in one corner and there were decorations and lights strung along the beams of the ceiling. December was low season for Bora Bora, but this bar was already full of people. To Kai and his family, it was a tourist venue that they tended to avoid, and he had chosen to meet Sienna here for that reason—he was less likely to be seen with her.

She looked up at the thatched ceiling of the

veranda. 'Honestly, I'm fascinated. I love the way this place sits on the beach as if it somehow grew here like the palm trees. And the cane furnishings are so stylish. It's all so harmonious. Is this a traditional Bora Bora building?'

'Built "in the style of" a *faré*, which is the traditional Tahitian house,' Kai said, making quote marks with his fingers.

'So not so authentic, then?'

'Authentic enough.'

'Forgive me. I'm an interior designer and I obsess with details sometimes. I'm meant to be having a holiday and not thinking at all about my work. But when I see something like this it's difficult to switch off.'

'That's understandable, if your work is important to you.'

For years his work had been the propelling force in his life, overwhelming everything else— including any kind of committed relationship. He'd had his heart broken when he was eighteen by an older woman, a guest at Mareva. It had been a doomed affair, but he hadn't seen that at the time. There had only ever been one other woman since who had seriously attracted him, a fun, smart Australian named Paige he'd met at a surfing tournament—but all she'd allowed him was a one-night stand and then she'd left him without even saying goodbye. Waking up to find she had gone had hurt; he hadn't really believed her when she'd said it could only be one night. For a long time he hadn't heard from her, and when he had seen her again it had been under very different circumstances. But he couldn't afford to wallow in heartbreak. He hadn't let himself get attached again.

His drive to prove himself had been relentless, not just to his parents but to the teachers who had expelled him from high school, and to certain others on the international surf circuit who had dismissed his ambitions. He'd lived out of a suitcase for so long he'd thought his life would always be like that. But a year ago everything had changed. Now he had responsibilities he had never foreseen.

'Being a workaholic is not desirable. In fact, it's downright unhealthy, according to my family,' Sienna said, with a downward quirk to her mouth. 'So I'll try not to spend my time inspecting the fittings and enquiring about the provenance of those stylish bamboo chairs.'

'Feel free to ask anything you like, although I'm no expert on chairs.' He did know an awful lot about the design of surfboards and the skills in marketing required to build a worldwide brand.

An awkward silence fell between them. The warm tropical air seemed thick with her unspoken questions. He had a few of his own he'd like to ask her.

They started to speak at the same time. 'I just wanted to ask—' she said.

'I wanted to tell you—' he started to say.

'Why I can't—'

'You need to know—'

She stared at him and they both dissolved into laughter. Her face flushed, her eyes sparkling, she was gut-wrenchingly beautiful. Again, he had that feeling of recognition that she could be important to him. Where it came from, he had no idea.

'You go first,' he said.

She took a sip of her drink then looked directly across the table at him. Her gaze was intense, her expression serious. 'The question—make that questions—I want to ask are first, why you can't give me a third kitesurfing lesson and second, why you asked to meet me so you could tell me about it.'

Thankfully, the waiter arrived then with their drinks, which gave Kai a few moments to collect his thoughts. He had not expected her to be so direct. Rather, he had been intending to introduce the subject in a more roundabout manner. Now he decided to simply tell the truth.

He leaned across the table to her. 'Because

I'm not a kitesurfing instructor. I've never been a kitesurfing instructor.'

She stilled with shock. 'What? No. You must be an instructor. You took me for two lessons. You were teaching those girls. I heard you.'

'Those girls are my nieces.'

'You weren't teaching them?'

'I was keeping an eye on them.'

'But I thought… I thought you were—'

'I know.'

She put her hands to her face to cover her eyes and bowed her head. 'I am so embarrassed.'

'Please don't be embarrassed. You weren't to know. For all intents and purposes, I must have seemed like an instructor. I'm sure I was giving the girls tips on how to improve their kitesurfing techniques.'

She looked up, her face flushed. 'Why didn't you tell me—? Why did you agree to—?'

'To teach you? Because I saw such intense longing in your eyes to be out there feeling the freedom and joy of flying across the water. Because you asked so nicely. Because I'm back home on Bora Bora for Christmas and I thought teaching a beautiful woman to kitesurf would be a pleasant way to spend some time. I didn't think a third lesson would be wise because I don't particularly care for deception, and it would be only too soon before someone who knew me saw us together and got curious.'

'Oh,' she said, confusion flitting across her features. 'So if you're not a kitesurfing instructor, who are you? Because you sure knew your stuff when it came to teaching this beginner.'

This was awkward but Kai didn't regret for a moment the hours he'd spent teaching Sienna and getting to know her without the hindrance of baggage or expectations. But he couldn't have let it go on any longer. He leaned across the table to get closer. He didn't particularly care to shout his personal business over the sounds of a busy bar.

'Getting back to the wetsuit you like so much... Did you notice the label?'

'I did. Wave Hunters. I recognised it because I've seen it on swimwear and fins. They sell that brand at the shop at the pool in London where I swim.'

'That's me. I'm Wave Hunters.'

From the perplexed look on her face, he might have chosen better words of explanation. 'I'm not sure what you actually mean by that, Kai.'

'I own the company.'

'You own Wave Hunters?'

'It started with a foldable, lightweight surfboard and grew from there.'

'When you say *grew* you mean, it's a big company?'

'One of the biggest,' he said, unable to stop a note of pride from entering his voice. 'We branched out from being known for surfing to encompass more water sports.' Although he said *we*, the company was all his; the people he worked with were employees not business partners.

'Including kitesurfing?'

'Yes. The equipment you've been using is all mine. Unbranded as yet, they're still prototypes. One of the reasons you picked up the sport so quickly—apart from your genuine natural aptitude—is that the board, kite and harness are all designed for optimum ease of use.'

'So the wetsuit really is a lucky one.'

'Actually, that's a well-established style. It sells in the store at your resort.'

'So I can buy it from there? Or do I pay you directly?' She reached for the small handbag she'd placed on the empty chair beside her.

'The wetsuit is yours,' he said. 'You don't have to pay. Put away your purse.'

'But Kai—'

'How could I possibly ask you to pay for a good luck wetsuit? A commercial transaction might strip it of its luck.'

A reluctant smile hovered around her lips. She really had the most beautiful mouth.

A very kissable mouth.

'You're teasing me. About the good-luck thing.'

'Am I? Can you afford to take the risk? About losing the good luck properties of that particular wetsuit, I mean.'

She laughed. 'You're not going to let me pay for it, are you?'

'No, I'm not.' The cost was nothing to him, but he couldn't say that without sounding arrogant. 'I know you wanted to buy the wetsuit as a gift to yourself, but you might have to accept it as a gift from me. You look fantastic in it. That means good publicity for Wave Hunters.'

'And the two lessons?'

He shrugged. 'Legally, I doubt I could charge you for lessons. But I wouldn't anyway. It really was my pleasure to teach you.'

'But I can't—'

'There's a third question you should ask me.'

'And that is?'

'Why did I agree to give you a second lesson?'

'Okay. I'll play. Why?'

'Because I wanted to see you again.' He paused. 'I really like you, Sienna.'

CHAPTER FOUR

SIENNA LIKED KAI TOO. She more than liked him. She was wildly attracted to him. Of course, she couldn't confess to that. All she could manage to do was choke out, 'Same. I mean, I like you too.'

But she could never admit that she'd fallen in *like* at first sight—and, yes, perhaps lust, too—when she'd seen him kitesurfing that first day at the beach. She'd accosted a businessman who was kitesurfing with his family and demanded he give her lessons. She cringed at the thought of it. But it seemed he hadn't minded. He hadn't minded at all.

For a long moment they looked at each other across the table, smiling. It was such an unexpected and wonderful moment, sincere, honest and just a touch awkward. How did she handle this?

'And… And I'd like to get to know you better,' she managed to get out, proud of herself for taking the initiative.

She wanted to know everything about him.

'I want to get to know you better too.' Sienna warmed to the sincerity in his deep brown eyes. She didn't care how she had met this man; she was just glad she had. He looked relaxed and at ease, dressed in casual white shirt and trousers—and was by far and away the best-looking man in the bar.

'However, I doubt I will surprise you with any revelations the way you have surprised me,' she said.

'Perhaps,' he said. His tone was enigmatic, and she realised how little she actually knew about him—and how much she wanted to know more.

'May I suggest right now we give the sunset our full attention?' he said. 'We can talk after.' She loved his French accent and the slightly formal way he had of speaking that made her aware that English was his second language even though he spoke it so perfectly.

'Agree,' she said.

Sienna watched in awe and wonder as, across from the lagoon, the sun started its descent behind the dark silhouette of Mount Otemanu, tinting the sky with its last rays in fiery streaks of pink, orange and red in breathtaking contrast to the turquoise tones of the water.

'People come from around the world to see this sunset. I never tire of it,' Kai said in a low, hushed tone.

'It's glorious,' she murmured. 'Almost other-worldly.'

This all seemed so unreal. Three days ago she was in London, wrapped in her winter coat and boots as she made her way home from a client's place in the dark drizzle of the evening to the family home in Chiswick, where she was temporarily living. Not that she didn't love London, of course she did, it was home, weather and all. But Bora Bora was a dream come true. Here she was in paradise, with this beautiful man who was turning out to be someone she felt at ease with, someone who wanted to get to know her like she did him. She had to blink hard to make sure she wasn't dreaming.

There was a collective sigh from the people in the bar as the sun disappeared. Everyone must have been like her, holding her breath at the beauty of it and then letting it out as the mountain receded into darkness. She was surrounded by canoodling couples again—the sunset was undoubtedly romantic. But she was with Kai—who knew if people thought they were a couple? It felt good not to be on her own after three days of standing out in her solitude.

She turned to Kai. 'I have no words.'

'And the best thing is we can watch it all again tomorrow evening.'

We? Did he mean him and her, or a general,

all-encompassing *we*? Would she see him again now that the kitesurfing lessons were no more?

'Nature's gift that keeps on giving.' It was an effort to keep her tone even when she was throbbing with awareness of him.

'That's the idea,' he said.

'I feel very close to nature here. I wish—' She stopped herself.

'What do you wish?'

'You know my sisters planned this vacation for me. I didn't know I was flying to Bora Bora until I was at the airport. There are…things I've always wanted to do, which I couldn't because… well, because.'

'You mean a bucket list?'

She nodded. 'You could call it that. Visiting a tropical island was near the top of the list, and my sisters helped me achieve that. I thought I could check off some others while I was here but now, I'm not sure and— Oh, never mind.'

'Can you share your bucket list with me?' Was she reading too much into his expression, imagining an intuitive understanding of what she hadn't said about why her list had remained unfulfilled throughout her marriage? 'Perhaps I could help you with it.'

There were some things on her bucket list that she would not share with Kai. It seemed she might now never achieve the first and most im-

portant item: *to have two children.* There was
another that she wouldn't share either: *to sleep
under the stars*—it seemed somehow too intimate.

'If you're sure?'

'Sienna, my work takes me around the world.
I grew up in Papeete. I have an apartment in
California at Huntington Beach.' She could just
close her eyes and listen to that sexy French accent. If she could, she would purr like her failed
foster cat, the one that had brought down the
Christmas tree and was still with her. 'However,
I'm in Bora Bora until the New Year to spend
time with my family before flying out again on
business. I can be your guide to make sure you
check some goals off your list.'

'That's kind of you,' she said, her heart giving an excited thud at the prospect of spending more time with him. 'I'm here until the day
after Christmas Day. It seemed a long time ahead
of me when I got here, but now it seems to be
shrinking rapidly. If you're sure you can spare the
time, I would love to take you up on your offer.'

Kai was about to reply when a young man,
blond and tanned, approached him. The man
nodded to Sienna before starting to speak in
French to Kai. Kai asked him to speak in English but she'd got the gist of the French—he
was an enthusiastic fan. Kai politely wound up

the conversation, and after much hand pumping the guy left.

'You've got quite an admirer there,' Sienna said. 'Wave Hunters must be very popular.'

Kai laughed. 'Before Wave Hunters I was a surfer. That's where he knows me from.'

'Not just any surfer by the sound of it.'

'I was a pro surfer on the international circuit.'

'I'm impressed. World class and famous in the surfing world. Do you compete in kitesurfing, too?'

He shook his head. 'Kitesurfing is purely for fun.'

Again, she cringed at the way she'd approached him for lessons, but she wouldn't apologise again. He'd made it clear he was okay with it. In fact, she was glad—she might never have met Kai otherwise. Or been given this chance to really get to know him.

'It was an exhilarating time of my life,' he said. 'And what I learned competing led directly to my success with Wave Hunters.'

'Your fan mentioned Teahupoo several times. Is that a person, or a place?' There had been something akin to reverence in the guy's voice.

Kai nodded slowly. 'Teahupoo is a famous Tahitian wave. One of the heaviest and potentially deadliest waves on the planet. It's also one of the most beautiful and awe inspiring. Big wave surfers from around the world come to test themselves against Teahupoo.'

'And you've surfed this scary-sounding wave?'

'I first surfed Teahupoo when I was thirteen years old. You won't find my name on any of the records, but I surfed it and there were witnesses.'

'That guy called you a legend. Are you a legend?'

'Some say so,' he said with the modesty she was beginning to recognise in him. 'But how do you define a legend?'

Just exactly who was Kai Hunter? There was so much more to him than she had imagined. She had a feeling there were more surprises to come. Not to mention an internet search as soon as she got back to her villa.

'Whatever way you define a legend, that guy was in awe of you.'

'He's an aspiring pro surfer. You understood him when he spoke French?'

'I speak some French, although nowhere near as well as you speak English. I regularly go to trade fairs in France and also seek out antiques and *brocante* for my clients. I need to be able to negotiate.'

Her shopping trips to the French flea markets seeking *brocante* finds were some of the most popular posts with her million-plus social media followers. That was the style she was applauded for: an eclectic placement of high-end designer with second-hand bargains, contemporary with vintage, making things seem on trend that had been consigned to oblivion in attics and second-hand stores. Domestic interiors were her specialty, with the fit out for fashionable restaurants and quirky boutiques being a sideline.

'Your work interests me,' he said. 'But first we need to look at your bucket list. I know this island very well and can perhaps be your guide.'

'Really? You'd do that?'

'You could get your goals checked off faster with my help.'

Sienna almost wished she hadn't mentioned the bucket list. The more she looked back at her marriage, the more she wondered why she had let Callum dominate her so much. Some of the 'to do' things on the list had been languishing there since before she was married. But she had been eighteen when she'd met him, with very little experience of men, and blinded by love. She'd believed there needed to be compromise in a marriage; however, from the get-go she had been the only one doing the compromising. It didn't reflect well on her that she'd allowed that to happen.

She would never let it happen again.

'Let me explain,' she said. 'I married quite

young, and my interests did not always align with my ex-husband's. So while I wanted to try kitesurfing and snorkelling, he wanted to ski. Or if I wanted to hike, he wanted to cycle.'

'So you learned to snowboard and cycle?'

'That's the way it went.'

When she'd first talked about getting married, her parents had warned her against it. 'I don't trust Callum and I'm not sure he always has your best interests front of mind,' her mother had said.

Needless to say, Sienna had been angry with them for interfering in her life. But it was only after she and Callum separated that her parents had revealed just how much they disliked him.

Thea and Eliza had never held back about how they felt about Callum. They'd been her bridesmaids, and just before they were about to walk up the aisle, they had urged her to pull out of the wedding if she had any doubts. Towards the end of her marriage, when it was apparent to her family how unhappy she had become, her sisters had shared the horrible nicknames they had devised for him. In the first years she would have chastised them—by the end she was ready to laugh with them.

'Are sailing and snorkelling on the bucket list?' Kai asked. 'Because I can certainly help you there.'

'Yes. So is kitesurfing. And surfing, though not on famous monster waves.'

'You've tried kitesurfing, so you can check that off your list.'

'No! I love it. I want to continue kitesurfing, every day if I can.' She paused. 'Only I'll have to find another instructor.'

'No need for that. You can kitesurf with me.'

'But you said—'

'Not as an instructor but as your friend and guide to the delights of Bora Bora.' She refused to let herself think about other delights that came to mind when she looked at Kai.

She smiled. 'I'd like that. Thank you.'

'As I said before, to learn to surf on this island is not ideal for a beginner. The best surf beaches for you to learn are on the island of Tahiti with the famous black sands. That's where I learned to surf.'

'But Tahiti is a long way from here. It took over an hour on the plane to get to Bora Bora from Papeete.'

'There is a ferry sometimes, that takes about seven hours.'

She frowned. 'I only have nine days left here. I don't want to spend an entire day of it travelling and another one back.'

'There is another alternative. There is a private island, Motu Puaiti, not far from Bora Bora where there's a sandy beach with a wave break ideal for a beginner surfer.'

'A private island? You can get permission to visit it?'

'That won't be a problem,' he said. 'If you want to learn to surf, I can take you. It's only a fifteen-minute ride by speedboat.'

'Yes, please, to the snorkelling and everything else. Where do I sign up?'

Kai thought Sienna's ex-husband sounded like a real jerk. Controlling, domineering and, reading between the lines, possibly even abusive. He didn't know the details of how the marriage had ended or how she had broken away—he didn't want to know. But the fact she was so determined to find her own way and live her own life rather than in her ex's shadow seemed to be a positive thing.

Not that he was an expert on relationships—far from it. His surfing career hadn't left room for commitment while he chased the waves all around the world. He couldn't be pinned down, didn't want to be pinned down. He'd needed all his energy, all his emotions, to ride the most challenging waves in the world and to fuel the ambition required to master them. Once he'd started Wave Hunters his focus had intensified on work to the exclusion of everything else. His foldup, fully recyclable, high-performance surf-board had been an immediate hit and when he and others started winning competitions on it, sales had soared far beyond expectations.

He'd always assumed that one day he would get married and have a family. He had always been very fond of his two nieces and nephew. But his lifestyle didn't do anything to help foster long-term relationships or thoughts of family. One more wave, one more exciting new product development for Wave Hunters—that always took priority. He'd had girlfriends, but his relationships ended either because his girlfriend at the time got tired of waiting for him to come back from yet another surf event, or he'd bailed when she'd started to hint about taking their relationship a step further. He just hadn't been ready.

There had been that one woman who'd captured his attention a few years back, at a time when he'd been feeling uncharacteristically lonely. Paige. He'd been in Sri Lanka to both guest judge a surfing event on the east coast and to visit with apparel manufacturers who supplied Wave Hunters. She was a physiotherapist attached to the Australian contingent of surfers, a few years older than he was, pretty, funny and elusive.

They'd flirted but it went no further until his

last day in Sri Lanka when she'd offered him one night—no strings, no 'keeping in touch;' just that one night. He'd gladly taken her up on her offer but had been surprised how sad he'd felt when he'd woken in his hotel room to find her gone. He'd felt a real connection—yet she had made it clear she didn't want to see him again and he had respected that. That hadn't stopped it hurting, though, and when he heard an Australian accent, it had reminded him of that hurt all over again.

Then a year ago someone had left a six-month-old baby girl in a basket at the reception desk of his grandparents' resort. There'd been a birth certificate naming Kai as the father and a note from the mother—Paige, the woman he'd had the one-night stand with in Sri Lanka—saying she loved Kinny but she could no longer look after her. The baby was well nourished, healthy and very, very cute. Her arrival had caused an uproar in the family and Kai had been barraged with questions—questions he'd struggled to answer. How did you explain a one-night stand to conservative parents? A DNA test had proved him to be her father. He'd doubted Paige would have lied about something so important, she'd seemed so straightforward, but he'd had to be certain.

His instant plunge into fatherhood had changed

Kai's life irrevocably. He fully accepted his responsibility for his child—that went beyond duty. But her care had become a juggling act. His grandparents doted on Kinny and were happy to have her live with them while he split his time between Bora Bora and travelling for work for extended periods. But while he loved Kinny— deep down he didn't feel like a 'proper' father. The way things were now, he was a visitor in her life. He wanted her to grow up with him as a constant presence. But he couldn't live on Bora Bora and run his international business. Solutions didn't come easily.

And now he had met a woman to whom he'd been instantly drawn. A woman who lived in London with a career of her own on the other side of the world. A woman who might baulk at discovering he came with baggage in the form of an eighteen-month-old toddler. He had to stop that thought from going any further. He was jumping the gun. He barely knew Sienna.

'Shall we plan a schedule for the next few days?' he said.

'Yes. Let's not waste a minute.' Again, he appreciated her enthusiasm and energy.

'My advice is to try snorkelling tomorrow in the lagoon here. The weather forecast is good. There are beautiful fish, stingrays and sharks to swim with.'

He waited for her reaction. She did not disappoint. First, she paled. Then she gulped. 'Sh-sharks? And… And stingrays?'

'Friendly ones,' he said.

'Is there any such thing as a friendly shark?'

'The blacktip reef sharks are quite small and timid. They won't approach you. They're used to people diving into their home waters and aren't bothered about us.'

'Are you sure about that?'

'You have to be sensible, no feeding them or patting them.'

He noticed Sienna did her best to suppress a shudder but didn't quite manage it. 'The last thing I could ever imagine doing is patting a shark.'

He laughed. 'Seriously. They're curious about you, and they're beautiful in their own way. Sharks are important in French Polynesian history and culture. They're actually a protected species here. There are bigger sharks, but they are out at sea past the lagoon and not known to be man-eaters.' Over the years and in waters around the world, he had encountered sharks but thankfully never an aggressive one.

'And the stingrays?'

'The stingrays have been part of our life here for so long we think of them as puppy dogs of the sea. You can pat them if you want.'

'I might pass on that.'

'Pass on the snorkelling?'

'No! Pass on patting the stingrays. I'll admire them from a distance.'

'Many people pat a Bora Bora stingray and live to tell the tale.'

'Not this person, thank you.' She sounded very British and commanding and it made him smile.

'How about I pick you up in my kayak at the dock at your resort at nine? Wear your wetsuit.'

'Okay. What about snorkelling equipment?'

'I'll bring what you need.'

'Thank you.' Her eyes shone with excitement. 'I can't wait.'

'We'll figure out the rest of your schedule over dinner.'

'Dinner?'

'I know we met for a drink but it's dinnertime now. The seafood is very good here. Would you join me for a meal?'

'Yes, please. I have to admit I'm starving.'

'Afterwards, I'll walk you back to your villa.'

He paused. He didn't want to tell her about his complicated family life. Not yet. Maybe never if nothing developed between them. But she was staying at Mareva and because of that their lives might intersect sooner than he'd like.

CHAPTER FIVE

NEXT MORNING KAI was at the resort dock, waiting for her when Sienna got there, along with his two-person blue kayak, beached on the sand nearby. It was, not surprisingly, emblazoned with the Wave Hunters logo.

Kai didn't notice her approach as he examined the end of one of the two kayak paddles and she had a quiet moment to observe and admire the man who occupied so much of her thoughts. He looked like a regular, too-handsome-to-be-true, ocean-loving French Polynesian guy, dressed in red-and-white-patterned board shorts and a black rash shirt. But he wasn't.

As soon as she'd got back to her villa the previous evening, a quick trawl through the internet had shown that Wave Hunters was a mega business, one of the biggest water sports brands in the world. And she'd asked him was his company *big*! Mentally, she banged her fist against her forehead. Kai Hunter was not just a legendary surfer but a billionaire. He was also known for his eligible bachelor status—a handsome billionaire with a home base in Los Angeles, frequent travels around the world, and never seen with the same girlfriend twice.

Scrolling from web page to web page last night she had felt rather foolish reading the full truth about the man she'd thought was a kite-surfing instructor. How ignorant he must have thought her. She felt flooded by the old self-doubt and insecurities Callum had done his best to foster. Why did someone like Kai want to spend so much time with her, helping her achieve the goals on her bucket list, when she certainly didn't move in the same circles?

He'd seriously downplayed his achievements and his reputation last night. But could she blame him for that? She would have thought him boastful if he'd labelled himself a billionaire tycoon. He'd been honest with her and hadn't played games.

I like you, he had said.

She hadn't played games either. So why did she feel suddenly shy at the prospect of being with him when she'd felt so at ease before?

Kai looked up at her and grinned. He put down the paddle and headed towards her. Her heart thudded into overdrive at the power of his smile. She had to battle those insecurities from getting the better of her and just enjoy his company.

'You're wearing the good luck wetsuit,' he said.

'I am. Hopefully, it has the power of protection against woman-eating sharks.' It was difficult to sound lighthearted when she now felt so self-conscious, and her words came out stilted.

'I'm sure it does,' he said, humouring her. 'The water is warm but you might be glad you're wearing a wetsuit if a stingray brushes against you.'

'Thanks for the warning,' she said with a shudder. 'Have you had to come far to pick me up?' For all their chat last night, she hadn't thought to ask where he lived on the island.

He paused. 'Not far at all. I stayed in this resort last night.'

She frowned. Why hadn't he told her that when, like a true gentleman, he'd escorted her to her villa?

'In a villa?'

He shook his head. 'Not as a guest. In an apartment reserved for my family. My grandparents own the Mareva resort. Last night we were talking so much I…well, I didn't get around to telling you.'

There was an edge to his voice that made her think he hadn't told her on purpose. She wondered why. There had been chemistry between them last night—she could practically feel it humming when they'd walked side by side to her villa. She hadn't wanted to say good-night; she'd been enjoying his company so much. And, yes, fantasising just a little about possible sexy scenarios starring him and her. But there had been no good-night kiss, no contact whatsoever. And that had been okay; she'd gone into her villa buzzing after her evening with him. She wouldn't dream of making the first move. Not when she'd had so much rejection from her ex. If anything was going to happen with Kai, it would happen when it was meant to—and only if he initiated it.

Kai most likely hadn't told her he was staying at the same resort because he was hyper-aware of guarding his privacy, being a billionaire bachelor and all. When it came down to it, they were still virtually strangers to each other.

'So…you live here? Your grandparents live here?' Had she been in contact with his grandparents without realising it? Maybe not. The staff she'd encountered had all been young.

'No to both questions. My grandparents live on a private island nearby. I have my own quarters there and stay with them when I'm on Bora Bora. However, it's sometimes more convenient to stay at Mareva. My *mama'u* and *papa'u* stay here quite often, although they don't work the hours they used to. I helped out here when I was a teenager so am used to staying in the family quarters when it gets too late to go home.'

Sienna noticed he hadn't mentioned his parents and she wondered why. But she didn't want to seem to be prying. The conversation the night before had been more general, about the wonderful food at the bar and other points about Bora Bora he had believed would interest her.

'Is that the private island you mentioned that's good for surfing?'

'No. A different one. There are many *motus* a short boat ride away from here.'

'*Motu* means island, right?'

'That's correct. A small island, a coral atoll. My grandparents live on a different *motu*. It's like a family compound. My brother, who lives in France, is also there for Christmas. The two girls you saw me kitesurfing with are his daughters.'

And the baby?

She didn't dare ask. There'd been no mention of a child in any of the media coverage of the billionaire owner of Wave Hunters. The teenage girls had picked the little toddler up and made a fuss of her after they'd finished kitesurfing; she was most likely their younger sister. Had the older couple been Kai's grandparents? She wished she'd looked more closely at them.

'A family Christmas,' she said. It was difficult not to sound wistful.

'Wherever I am in the world, I always come home to Bora Bora for Christmas. It pleases my grandparents.'

Obviously not just because it was a paradise, but because he wanted to be with his family. She liked that. Callum hadn't been close to his family although he worked for his father's property development company. They'd seemed close— that closeness was one of the things that had appealed to her about marrying him. Yet it had been superficial. In fact, a fierce rivalry had developed between Callum and his brother, as the father played them off against each other. Of all the years they'd been together, only twice had there been a conflict of family obligation on Christmas Day. The Reeves family didn't make much of an effort for Christmas or indeed birthdays, and Callum thought the Kendall family overdid it. When Callum's sister had her first baby, he hadn't been nearly as excited as Sienna had been. Excited and longing for the day when she would hold her own baby in her arms. But a baby had always been put in the 'not yet' basket by her ex. Until he'd bluntly told her it was never going to happen—he didn't want children.

'What a wonderful place to come home to,' she said with a wave that encompassed the thatched buildings and riot of bright tropical flowers of the resort, the beauty of the lagoon.

'I can relax here,' he said. 'People know me for who I am. I don't have to pretend otherwise.'

She couldn't, just couldn't, think of anything else to say. An awkward silence fell between them.

'Are you okay?' he said. He stood close, looking down at her, exploring her face—and she didn't feel she could hide how she felt from him.

'Yep. Fine. I...I... Well, about last night. And our revelations. I didn't know how huge and important Wave Hunters is and that...that you're a billionaire.'

'You did some internet surfing.'

'Yes.'

'Does that change how you feel about me taking you snorkelling?'

'Of course not. Why would it?' She couldn't confess to feeling just the teeniest bit intimidated by what she'd learned about him online.

'The media might call me a 'billionaire bachelor' but it's just a label.'

'The billionaires I've encountered in my work haven't been particularly nice.'

'Don't judge me on them. I'm still the same person who taught you kitesurfing. Still the same person who shared the wonder of the sunset with you.' He paused, looked closer, and a shiver of awareness ran through her. 'The same person who is very much enjoying getting to know you.'

Her doubts and fears melted away under the intensity of his gaze. 'Me too. I mean, I'm really enjoying getting to know you.' Having him stand this close was making her feel giddy. She could drown in those deep chocolate eyes. He took a step back and the air between them suddenly felt empty. She almost staggered at the loss.

'You weren't the only one to do an internet search,' he said.

'You looked me up?'

'I'm seriously impressed. Not only are you a social media influencer with more than a million followers hanging on to your every word on how to make their rooms look better, you also used to work with one of the most prestigious, long-standing design companies in the UK.'

That always looked good on her CV. 'I had an internship with them, then was fortunate enough to get a full-time job.'

'Not just good fortune. You must have been very good.'

His words threw her for a moment. She had got so used to being put down by Callum in the dying years of their marriage. But she rallied her self-esteem. 'I was. I am.'

Her first instinct was to downplay her talents and achievements. But she was learning to own them and trumpet them. Her sister Thea told her she had to be her own number-one fan. 'It was a marvellous experience and the prestige of working for them has done me nothing but good. But ultimately, I developed my own style and it clashed with the more traditional look that the company favoured.'

'Was it difficult to leave?'

'At times I wondered had I done the right thing, but I've never regretted it. If you've seen my socials, you might know I started with a video documenting the renovation of my first apartment, while doing some freelance work. The apartment was in much worse condition than I had imagined when we bought it. A wall nearly collapsed on me when I stripped off the layers of wallpaper that went right back to Edwardian times. I made a funny video of it and it went viral. Before I knew it, I had clients as well as followers and my own business, Sienna Kendall Design.' She had never used her married name of Reeves when it came to work. 'I never looked back.'

'Now your sisters are making sure you take a break. I bet it's difficult for you not to check in to your business while you're here.'

'You are so right. I've scheduled posts for while I'm away so I don't lose my rankings but it's like an addiction. What about you?'

'I can never tune out of Wave Hunters. I have an excellent executive team but the buck always stops with me.'

'Even in Bora Bora?'

'Especially in Bora Bora, when I can't be hands-on. I have to spend a good part of my time online.'

'Except when you're teaching me to kitesurf.'

'And snorkel. And anything else where you need my talents to help you.'

The thought flashed through her mind of a new addition to her bucket list: *have mind-blowing sex with a gorgeous, kind man.*

She suspected Kai might have some exciting talents in that direction. She had never felt so attracted to a man. She looked down and scuffed the sand with her toes for fear he might see her thoughts on her face. Then took a deep breath to steady herself, to make her voice sound normal rather than laced with longing.

'Talking about snorkelling, before you ask, I do know how to kayak,' she said. 'One of my uni friends came from the Lakes District. One summer break, a group of us went up there and kayaked around the lakes. We had a ball. I loved it.' Only Callum hadn't. So she hadn't kayaked again, despite repeated invitations from her friend. Of course she'd lost touch with her, until the news of her divorce had got out and that friend had got in touch to congratulate her.

Kai handed her a paddle. 'That's great news. Let's get out on the lagoon. I'll show you how to fit your mask and snorkel and we'll be off.'

The sun filtered down in golden shafts through the crystal-clear aquamarine water, making patterns on the white sand below; luminous green water plants gently waved in the current; and myriad colourful fish darted among the coral. Snorkelling in the Bora Bora lagoon with Kai was so amazing, Sienna couldn't find superlatives enough to describe it. Kai swam close to guide her and point out interesting things under the water, and she noticed with a tremor of awareness every time his legs nudged hers or his hand slid past her body with his stroke. There was something surreal about being in the water together with no words exchanged.

She quickly got the hang of breathing through the snorkel and just a flip of the long fins sent her gliding effortlessly through the water. When she and Kai surfaced after a deep dive, she blew water out of her snorkel as he had taught her, then took out the mouthpiece, treading water to stay afloat.

'Why haven't I ever done this before? I've always wanted to. It's like a different world down there. This place is paradise under the water as well as on land. And you're right. The reef sharks just ignore us and I'm not frightened of them at all. Although the first sight of a shark fin coming towards me struck terror in my heart and had the theme music from *Jaws* echoing in my ears. Even the stingrays are sweet in their own way. And I couldn't believe it when that cormorant spear-dived into the water near me to catch a fish.' She paused. 'Sorry, I'm gabbling.'

He smiled, a slow, easy smile. 'No need to apologise for your excitement. I like it. You're very cute.'

Cute? He found her cute? Even through his mask she could see his eyes were warm with genuine admiration and an interest that went beyond that of an instructor. Instinctively, she swam nearer until they were even closer. The fins made it easy.

'I think you're cute, too,' she said. 'Well, not *cute*…you're too big for cute—*impressive*, yes, impressive.' What she really wanted to say was that he was absolutely gorgeous and the sexiest man she'd ever met. However, she didn't feel she knew him well enough to say that. But she felt so at home in the water, so at home with *him*. It seemed a long moment that they looked into each other's faces, smiling.

Then he reached over and, using both hands,

took off her mask, sliding it over her head, sending shivers of sensation through her. Startled, she did the same for him, though her hands weren't quite steady at such an intimate touch on his face. She started to say something, but he cupped her face in his hands and kissed her. In the middle of a lagoon while they were treading water to keep afloat, holding on to their masks and snorkels, he kissed her. It was totally unexpected but after only a second's hesitation she kissed him back. His mouth was warm and he tasted of salt water. It was a tender, exploring kind of kiss, with gentle pressure and a light caress of the seam of her mouth with his tongue. Yet, tender as it was, it was also incredibly sensual. The added sensation of being together in the water, with his hard body supporting her, lifted the kiss to an exciting intensity.

It was an unusual place to share a first kiss, but it seemed just right, and she felt a slowly bubbling excitement at the thought of what might come next.

She wanted him.

Truth be told, she'd wanted him from the first time she saw him. And now she had grown to respect and like him—and like and lust made a formidable combination. Finally, it became too difficult to stay afloat and kiss and they slid under the water. She broke away from him as they surfaced, laughing and spluttering.

'That was fun,' she said.

'I've wanted to kiss you since your kitesurfing lesson,' he said.

'The first lesson, or the second one?'

'The first one.'

'Good, now I can admit I wanted to kiss you on that first lesson too. I didn't expect it to be while we were swimming, though.'

'We learn new skills every day,' he said, and that made her laugh.

'I'm loving the snorkelling—and the kissing too,' she said, which earned her another swift kiss.

A small boat with snorkellers and a tour guide came near, and Sienna pulled away from Kai, suddenly self-conscious. The tour guide knew Kai and waved to him, and they exchanged greetings in French.

Kai put his arm around her and pulled her close for a quick hug. 'We have company,' he said in a low voice. 'Shall we resume our lesson rather than being the main attraction for the tourists?'

'Good idea,' she said, grateful for his understanding.

'You have an affinity for water sports,' he said. 'Is scuba diving on your bucket list? Because if you like snorkelling this much, you'll love what you see out in the open waters away from the lagoon.'

'To be honest, I hadn't considered it. But scuba is going on the list now.'

'The sooner you tick off one goal from your bucket list, you add another.'

'Funny like that, isn't it?' she agreed.

Do not think about the 'mind-blowing sex' goal on the list.

That kiss had made her hungry for more kisses, more caresses, more Kai.

'Scuba is where you need an accredited instructor and there're excellent schools here. But it takes time, at least three days.'

'Which sadly I don't have, not if I want to do other things while I'm here.'

Next time, she almost said, before swallowing the words.

Would there ever be a next time for her in Bora Bora? She'd been looking on this trip as a once-in-a-lifetime event, which was why she was so hungry to experience everything the island had to offer.

And now there was Kai. This might be all the time she would ever have with him. She had to make the most of every single minute without tripping herself up by anxiety of where it might go.

CHAPTER SIX

FOR THE FIRST time since he'd launched Wave Hunters, Kai resented the demands it made on his time. More specifically, the time he would prefer to spend with Sienna. He thought about her constantly. He wanted to spend every moment he could with her.

He was obsessed with her.

He'd never met anyone like Sienna Kendall, never felt this way about any other woman. And he was only too aware that her time here on the island was limited and ticking rapidly away. He didn't know where this attraction between them would lead to, but he wanted it to lead *somewhere*, even if it was just a memorable fling. That brief, irresistible kiss in the water with her had ignited desire for her that had been smouldering since the first day he'd met the beautiful woman in the bronze bikini.

He hadn't seen her since the day they'd snorkelled in the morning and kitesurfed in the afternoon, before he'd had to go home to attend to Wave Hunters business and spend time with his precious Kinny. His baby girl was growing so fast, it sometimes seemed there were changes every day. He was finding it more and more difficult to be away from her.

But today was allocated to Sienna. He wouldn't let anything stand in the way of this day with her. Success in life for Kai had come with total commitment to his goal. In big wave surfing, if you didn't commit to the wave—choose it, focus, go for it with everything you had—you could be taken out, injured, even killed. To be a billionaire by the age of thirty in a highly competitive market meant being totally driven to the exclusion of everything else. He had never given a relationship with a woman anything like that level of commitment. Until now, he hadn't wanted to. Now he was ready to make Sienna his, even if it was only until the day after Christmas, when she would head back to her life in London. He couldn't let himself think further than that. Not yet.

This morning he was taking her to Motu Puaiti so she could try surfing for the first time. He was impatient to see her. So impatient he arrived early at the resort to pick her up. He strode down the pathway to the wooden dock, which led out into the lagoon and branched off from both sides to the individual thatched roof private villas. Heart pounding, he willed his steps to get him faster to Sienna. He needed to see her to reassure himself she was still here, that these feelings were real. That he hadn't imagined she might feel the same. Hell, he just wanted to see her.

He buzzed at her doorway. Then buzzed again when she didn't answer. Finally, she opened the door to him, dressed just in a short, white cotton wrap, her hair wet and dripping onto her shoulders.

All he could do was stare. Hungrily, he took in every detail, the way the wrap gaped open to reveal the swell of her high, firm breasts, her long, toned legs, how utterly lovely she was without makeup. She was beautiful and he wanted her. Not just to make love with her, although that was foremost in his mind, but to spend time with her in the rare companionship they had so quickly established.

'You're early,' she said with a slow smile. 'I've been for a quick swim in the lagoon from the ladder off the deck and I was in the shower.'

He had to suppress a groan at the thought of her naked in the shower, twisting and turning to soap her luscious body.

'I know I'm early,' he said. 'I couldn't wait any longer to see you.'

Their gazes locked. He saw the longing he felt for her echoed in her extraordinary green eyes. Again, he had that sensation of connection, of inevitability, of *possibilities*. The world seemed to slip away. Sounds became magnified: the water lapping against the supporting structures of the villa, the cry of a sea bird, the rapid increase of her breath, the pounding of his own heart.

'I…I missed you,' she said, her voice a low murmur.

'I missed you, too,' he said, his heart soaring with joy that she felt the same way. 'Every moment I wasn't with you, I missed you.'

Then the distance between them closed as they both stepped towards each other. At last, he had her in his arms, warm and pliant. He sighed an audible sound of relief. This is where he wanted to be. With her. *Sienna.*

He kissed her, grateful that this time they were on dry land and didn't have the distraction of an audience of tourists to get in the way, and she kissed him back, tentatively at first, and the thought crossed his mind she might be out of practice. But she very soon relaxed into it with a little murmur of pleasure. She wound her arms around his neck to bring him closer, pressed her mouth against his. He didn't pressure her, making his kiss gentle but firm until her enthusiastic response saw it rapidly escalate into something more passionate, her tongue answering his. She had nothing on under that robe and he could feel her nipples pebbling against his chest, even through his T-shirt. They kissed for a long time. He slid his hands down her sides, brushing past the sides of her breasts.

Too much, too soon? She pulled away, panting. 'Wow. Just wow. I wasn't expecting that to be so intense. I loved it but—'

'As you know, I've wanted to kiss you properly since that first day. And our brief kiss yesterday did nothing to dampen that desire.'

'Me too, I mean, I've wanted to kiss you, be kissed by you—you know what I mean.'

He kissed her again, long and sweet and sensual. He broke the kiss but held her tight in the circle of his arms.

'I wanted to take it slowly, getting to know you,' he said. 'But time is racing away from us. We need to get to know each other more quickly.'

And that meant telling her about Kinny.

Because he and Kinny came as a package deal.

'Yes. Yes.' She reached up to kiss him once again. He loved the taste of her, the feel of her body close to his, the subtle scent of *tiare*, the Tahitian gardenia, on her skin from the bathroom products favoured by the resort.

'We have the entire day today to spend on

Puaiti. We could stay overnight there if you would like, if that isn't pushing you too quickly—'

'Yes. No. I mean, *yes*, I would like to stay overnight. You're not pushing too quickly.'

'Staying the night doesn't mean you have to—'

She put up a finger across his mouth to silence him. He kissed it. 'It can mean whatever we want it to mean,' she said, her voice husky. He felt a rush of excitement and anticipation at her words.

She turned away, treating him to a view of the wrap that barely covered her behind. Did she realise how desirable she was? He had a feeling her ex had done a number on her confidence. She deserved so much better.

'I packed a bag for going off island and my lucky wetsuit,' she said. 'Now I'll have to pop in a few more things I'll need for overnight. I need to get dressed, too, of course.' She looked up at him. He liked that hint of mischief that often laced her smile.

'You look very good in what you have on,' he said, his voice husky.

She tugged self-consciously at the hem of her wrap to pull it down. He wished she wouldn't; he liked the way the wrap opened and rode up to reveal tantalising glimpses of her naked body. 'More to the point, what I don't have on,' she said with a laugh. 'I wasn't expecting company just yet.' She paused. 'But I was counting the minutes until you got here.'

'Me also.' He gritted his teeth against an offer to help her get dressed. They'd never leave this room if he did. 'I'll wait out on your deck for you.'

The glass viewing platform, set into the floor of the deck, gave a window to the waters of the lagoon below. Kai watched the colourful, striped fish dart in and out of the coral and waving water plants. He decided to count them, anything to distract himself from thoughts of Sienna slipping out of that robe and sliding into her underwear. Did she wear sexy underwear or practical underwear? Being strong and sporty she might prefer practical, although she was also a designer and that gave him hope for slinky and sexy. He didn't really care, because if he was to get into the fortunate situation where he saw her dressed just in her underwear, his only thought would be to strip it off her ASAP.

He had counted to fish number two hundred and seventeen when Sienna emerged. She wore long white shorts, sandals and a coral-coloured T-shirt with a pineapple print on the front. She noticed him looking at it and did a little model twirl. Had any woman looked as sexy in such casual clothes?

'Cute, isn't it? It's new. I took the shuttle bus from the resort into Vaitape yesterday to do some shopping. I bought the T-shirt, this woven pandanus straw hat, which I'll wear today, and this bag, which I love. I also bought some gifts for my family and friends.'

'Gifts for yourself, too, I'm sure.'

'Of course. The hand-painted *pareos* were so beautiful, I bought one for each sister and one for myself.'

'Not to be gift wrapped?'

'And not a surprise,' she said with a laugh.

'What else did you see there?'

'Galleries with some striking paintings and photography, but everything I liked was too bulky to take home with me.'

'You made some good buys,' he said. He would take her shopping again, and ship anything she wanted to send to London via Wave Hunters.

'It was fun,' she said. 'I had lunch with an older couple staying here at my resort on their second honeymoon. We met on the shuttle bus. Then in the afternoon I cycled around the island. It didn't take long.' She paused, looked up into his face. 'But I would've preferred to have been kitesurfing with you.'

He stilled. 'I would have preferred that too,' he said. 'But work was unavoidable.' He'd cursed the time away from her. It was the first time he would rather have been with a woman than dealing with production problems or finessing a new design.

'Of course it was. I totally understand that,' she said.

Being a businesswoman herself, he was sure she did. Another thing he really liked about Sienna was she was so independent. She had insisted on paying for her share of her meal at the beach bar the other night. Of course he hadn't let her, but he'd appreciated her attitude. Too many people expected him to pay for everything just because he could.

He took her bag from her. 'But today is the day we check off another goal from your bucket list. Conditions are ideal for you to learn to surf.'

She clapped her hands together in that enthusiastic way he liked so much. 'I'm looking forward to it.'

As he ushered her out the door before him, he put his hand on her waist. When they headed towards the dock where the speedboat was moored, he took her hand in his. She looked up at him and smiled while she answered the pressure of his hand with hers. He didn't care who saw them.

His presence with Sienna on the lagoon had been duly noted and reported to his grandmother. Kai and the only single woman of eligible age staying at Mareva was big news in his immediate family circle. Not that there was anything untoward in the report to Mama'u. On the contrary, she would be delighted he was seeing someone. She thought at thirty-five he was too old to be single. Especially when he now had a child. However, he knew his grandmother would prefer the woman who had caught his interest not to be a transient guest at the hotel who might hurt her beloved grandson.

Mama'u had been there for him the time an older woman staying at Mareva had lured him as a teenager into an affair and broken his young heart. The woman had been married and toying with him but at the time the pain had been real. He'd made sure his heart had never been broken again—even by Paige—that would have distracted him from his goals. His grandmother would say he'd gone too far, cutting himself off from emotional attachments, But the unexpected joy of having Kinny in his life had thawed a part of his heart he'd thought long frozen. Meeting Sienna made him realise there might be more he was missing out on, that his life was empty in some ways. His grandparents were wise, tolerant and loving and if they gave counsel, he listened to them. Unlike his parents, they always had his interests at heart.

If it went well for him with Sienna on Puaiti, he would invite her to meet his family on the nearby larger *motu* where they lived, and introduce her to Kinny.

As Kai had told her, the trip by speedboat to the private *motu* of Puaiti only took fifteen minutes. Fifteen minutes of exhilarating speed through turquoise waters reputed to be the most beautiful in the world—a claim Sienna would not dispute—and they arrived at a small, postcard-perfect island ringed by sugar-white sand and fringed with palm trees. The sky was a breathtaking cloudless blue, and again that word *paradise* came to mind. It hardly seemed real.

Kai pulled up at the long wooden dock and killed the motor. 'This is it,' he said. 'We have the *motu* all to ourselves.'

'The owner doesn't mind?'

'The owner is very pleased to have you here.'

The way Kai said that made her look sharply up at him. 'Do you know them? Don't tell me your grandparents own this island, too?'

He looked very serious. 'I told you I hadn't finished with revelations about me and my life.' He paused. 'I own this island.'

'You? Seriously? Your own personal paradise island?'

She felt like she'd moved into some alternate

universe where guys her age owned private islands in one of the most expensive parts of the world. Kai was seriously minted. She'd made money flipping apartments in London—also an expensive part of the world—but she couldn't even begin to imagine what this island would be worth. Or how wonderful it would be to own it.

'The previous owners of the island had to sell in a hurry and I snapped it up. Very wealthy couple, very nasty divorce. They planned to have it as their holiday home and develop a small, exclusive resort. Nothing came of it.'

'Is there a house on it?'

'A dated house built by the first owners, a French family. But it's liveable. They planned to knock it down. The couple I bought the island from made a few changes to the house but never actually lived in it before they had to sell.'

'What do you intend to do with it?'

His own personal island.

'Make it my home, perhaps. Have a beginner's surfing school here, maybe. The next *motu* to the east is my grandparents' place. You can see it in the distance. At the moment, however, just to own this place is enough.'

'Of course it is,' she said, feeling a tad overwhelmed. Again, she was reminded how different their lives were in every way. Yet when she'd been in his arms, when he'd been kissing her, none of that had mattered. All that mattered was him and how he made her feel and how she hadn't wanted him to stop. How she was looking forward to spending the night here with him.

'I know you have a thing about billionaires and—'

'I don't have a thing about billionaires. And I certainly don't have a thing against you. I wouldn't put a label on you, Kai.'

He picked up her hand and kissed it. Such a simple gesture, yet so heartwarming and pleasurable, tingles of awareness shooting through her.

'I'm glad to hear that,' he said. 'I don't like to be labelled.'

'I kinda sensed that,' she said. 'Not that I actually know any billionaires. Not to socialise with, that is. But my job at the design company took me inside the homes of the very wealthy. One country house that was considered quite modest had seventeen bathrooms. It's where I got to be wary of billionaires. The old ones I encountered were arrogant and very entitled. The young ones had inherited money and added to that list of attributes by being sleazy.'

'Obviously not representative of hardworking, self-made people,' he said.

'Like you.'

'And you. You're quite the entrepreneur.'

Own your achievements.

She could almost hear her sister Thea in her ear.

'Yes, I am successful, and proud of it,' she said.

'So you should be,' he said.

He helped her off the boat and onto the dock. 'I can't wait to get that sand between my toes and get out in that surf,' she said. She looked up at him. 'You know I wouldn't dare do this without you beside me. It's all too much out of my comfort zone to do it by myself.'

CHAPTER SEVEN

SIENNA FOLLOWED KAI up a pathway, scattered with fallen palm fronds, to the house—*his* house—which he told her hadn't been lived in for some years. She'd been expecting something humble, a beach shack—tumbledown even— and was shocked at the reality of the luxurious architect-designed house in perfect condition.

'It's like a time capsule from the nineteen sixties,' she said, looking around at the decep- tively simple design, spacious, perfectly propor- tioned rooms with polished wooden floors and floor-to-ceiling windows designed to capture the views every way she looked.

'Very hip at the time, I believe,' Kai said.

'And back in fashion now too.' The retro fur- niture would fetch quite a hefty sum in the auc- tion rooms of London.

'There was an original old wooden structure, which was demolished when a very wealthy French family of industrialists commissioned this house to be their private retreat for themselves and their family. They came here each year for many years. Sadly, their only grandchild died in an accident in Paris and they were so grief stricken they never came back.'

'What a tragedy,' she said, disconcerted.

She could almost feel the hopes and dreams for this place that had died with that child. It was a reminder she needed to take life's chances while she could. Her family had had to manage their recurrent fear that they might lose Eliza, and the Christmas pact in part had sprung from that—a brave new start not just for now healthy Eliza but for all of them.

Thank you, lovely sisters, for sending me here to Bora Bora—and to Kai.

'Only a caretaker lived here. The couple I bought the island from kept him on while they figured out what to do with the property,' Kai said.

'What a waste of such a marvellous house. But it explains why it's in such good condition.'

He ran his finger down a wooden window frame. 'You need to be vigilant about the upkeep of a building so close to the sea. Wind and salt can be very damaging. Upkeep of an island is very expensive.'

'So worth it. I can't believe the first owners wanted to tear this down.' Sienna stroked the back of a wonderful mid-twentieth-century rattan chair, one of a pair. 'What happened to the caretaker?'

'He retired.'

'Who looks after the house now?'

'One of my grandmother's housekeepers and her husband. Let's check the refrigerator. She should have stocked it with food and drinks for our stay.'

He mentioned it so casually, almost a throwaway comment. As if everyone had a fleet of housekeepers at their disposal. How different their lives had been.

The kitchen had obviously had some alterations done over the years, but they'd been done well. The refrigerator, a modern one, was stocked with seafood, fruit, salads and cold drinks. 'I guess we won't be needing the water and snack bars I've got in my bag,' she said. She hadn't known what to expect of the day.

'Thank you but no, we won't go hungry here.'

She wondered about the facilities of this tiny island all on its own in the Pacific Ocean. 'Is there fresh water on the island?'

'A coral-filtered well and rain-collection tanks.'

'Solar panels for electricity?'

'Yes. And satellite for communications.'

'What a fabulous, fabulous place,' she said,

turning around to view every angle of the room. 'I absolutely love it.' She was used to seeing inside splendid homes in London and didn't often feel envy, but this place was something altogether special. She would dream about it when she got back home.

'I knew when I saw the island that it had to be mine,' Kai said. 'Although the house needs some refurbishing. I'm sure your professional eye would see that.'

'I would keep refurbishment to the minimum. The place is perfect in so many ways.'

'Wait until you see the bathrooms,' he said wryly.

Sienna smiled. 'Okay, I'll reserve my professional opinion until then. Let me have a look.' She made her way to the nearest bathroom.

'You're absolutely right,' she said, when she came back into the living area, pretending to stagger. 'I would advise a total remodelling of that bathroom. I wish I'd had my sunglasses with me to cope with the clashing, patterned tiles and the coloured sanitary ware. I think they've burned my retinas. Who knew they made bright yellow handbasins and toilets in those days?'

He grinned. 'I thought you might think that.'

'The thing with an old house is to respect its past while giving it a stylish future. The bathroom tiles and fittings are a historical conversation piece but really aren't compatible—funky as they are—with what we expect of a bathroom today.'

'Which is a diplomatic way of saying they're awful. Functional but ugly.'

'That about sums it up.'

You had to be careful about criticising a client's home. She'd learned that early in her career. Not that Kai was a client. She couldn't even call him a friend. Could he come to mean something to her? Had he already? She flushed at the thought of those heady kisses in the villa when he'd come to pick her up. She was so tempted to tell him to skip the surfing lesson and lead her down to the bedroom for lessons of an altogether different kind.

'The other five bathrooms are the same,' he said.

'Six bathrooms?'

'There are five bedrooms each with its own bathroom.'

'The house is bigger than it looks from first impressions. Can I have a quick look at the other bathrooms?'

'Go ahead.'

The other bathrooms were indeed similar to the first one she'd seen with variations in colour. The bedrooms were spacious and airy, with stylish cane and rattan furniture, plantation shutters and ceiling fans, but could do with some refreshing in terms of soft furnishings. While clean, there was a general air of disuse except for the main bedroom, which she assumed was used by Kai when he visited. She didn't linger in his bedroom, which contained a new king-size bed that triggered a flurry of fantasies of Kai, his magnificent body naked, inviting her to join him. She shuddered a little in anticipation.

It was a family-size house. A house for children, their laughter echoing through all the rooms. She felt that familiar stab of pain at the thought of the years she'd spent married to a man who had let her believe she would have children and then reneged in such a cruel way. Now she feared she would never achieve that number-one goal on her bucket list.

She didn't want to marry again—it would take years to ever trust a man and by then she might be too old—and she couldn't imagine having a baby on her own. Yet life without children seemed a life half lived—for her anyway. People called her foster cats her 'child substitutes,' not seeing the hurt such comments caused her. Even the most beloved cat was no substitute for a baby.

She came back into the main room, walked to the window, looked out to the view of the sea framed by palm trees that leaned down to the water, then turned back to face Kai. 'You know, I sometimes get a feeling about a house.'

'Do you have a feeling about this house?'

'Yes. Very strongly. This house was built with love—and it's waiting to be loved again.'

'An interesting observation,' he said. She was glad he didn't laugh at her.

She shrugged. 'I feel it. That doesn't mean I can explain it.' So much of designing for other people involved intuition. She wondered if her 'feelings' were a heightened sense of intuition that almost veered into the spooky.

'What were the bathrooms telling you?'

'Rescue us!' she said with a laugh.

She knew exactly how she would like to design the bathrooms. Her mind even tripped into work mode about how the materials would be delivered to the island. Boat? Helicopter? A crazy thought came to her that perhaps one day Kai could engage her to do the design work and she could come back to Bora Bora. But that was simply too unrealistic a thought to give it any head room. *Just enjoy today*, she urged herself. *And tonight.*

There was no point in thinking any further than that. Whatever might happen with her and Kai could only be a holiday fling.

She'd brought her phone with her. How she would love to post photos of these rooms on her socials after she got home. Later, she would ask him if he would mind.

'Are you ready to surf?' he said.

'I'm ready to give it a go, that's for sure. Especially when I'm to be taught by a legendary surfing champion.' He smiled at that.

'You need to get into that lucky wetsuit,' Kai said.

'I'll get changed in the bathroom. This time I'll take my sunglasses in with me.'

Kai collected two large, long surfboards and two much smaller bodyboards from a storeroom that led off the side veranda. Sienna noticed snorkelling equipment inside the storeroom and some stylish beach chairs, loungers and fold-up cabanas—no doubt additions from the most recent previous owners.

Kai handed her the bodyboards, while he carried the larger boards, and she followed him away from the house through to a small, idyllic, crescent-shaped beach, lined by palm trees which grew right to the water's edge. They walked on the sand, warm and gritty beneath her bare feet. The sound of the waves crashing onto the beach was loud and rhythmic and she could smell the salt in the air. This part of the world was so beautiful it literally took her breath away.

'See how evenly the waves are rolling in, and

how gently and slowly they break?' Kai said. 'They don't get any higher than a metre, which I'm sure you can handle.'

Even though Kai said they were small, the waves looked quite large to her. But she had an expert teacher by her side.

'I'll do my best,' she said.

'The conditions are ideal. And you won't have to worry about other surfers. The beach is ours.'

'Literally, the beach is yours,' she said, still marvelling at the truth of it.

'And I'm sharing it only with you,' he said, as he dropped a quick kiss on her mouth. Just that touch was enough to flood her with desire for this gorgeous-in-every-way man. She wanted to hold him close for more kisses but was still too uncertain of what their status was to take the initiative. After all, they had only kissed properly for the first time this morning. And she was so out of practice with dating.

'I appreciate the honour, I truly do,' she said.

Some of the super-luxurious hotels on Bora Bora owned private *motus* for their guests' use, the most famous of which was probably Motu Tapu. She had the privilege of being the sole visitor to this most perfect private *motu*. And all because she'd screwed up the courage to ask Kai Hunter—*the* Kai Hunter—to teach her how to kitesurf.

'Have you used a bodyboard before?' Kai said.

'No. I'm a complete novice in the surf.' She looked up to him. 'I'm totally in your hands.'

'I like the idea of that,' he said, his voice husky. For a long moment their gazes locked, and she saw the same flare of interest and awareness she'd registered that morning in her villa room.

His hands were large and strong, with long, well-shaped fingers. This morning she'd had a brief taste of how good they felt on her body. A shiver of anticipation ran through her at the thought of what more he could do if she gave herself over to his hands. 'Uh…me too,' she managed to choke out. 'I mean, I know you'll look after me in the water.' She could only anticipate how he might look after her in the bedroom— or the living room, against the wall, *anywhere*.

'Count on it,' he said. Was there a second meaning there? Or had he switched into surfing-instructor mode? 'A bodyboard is a good place to start. It's easy to manoeuvre, you lie on it rather than standing up and it's easier to get the feel for catching and riding a wave.'

She followed him down to the water, unable to resist admiring his back view along the way. Could there be a more perfect male body? He really was insanely attractive in every way. Not for the first time, she wondered why he was single, was glad he was.

He fastened a leg strap to her ankle that connected to the bodyboard. 'This is so you don't lose your board if you come off. You also don't want your runaway board to hit other people in the water. Of course, that doesn't apply here.'

They had this entire island to themselves. It seemed somehow surreal. Could you get any farther away from the busy streets of London? Holding the board under her arm, she pushed through into the water until it became waist high. Kai showed her how to get onto the board and paddle out past the waves.

'I'm taking in quite a lot of water,' she spluttered.

'That's to be expected. Paddling is hard work and takes a lot of upper-body strength. But you'll get into the rhythm of it.'

It seemed like forever before they got out past the breakers but Sienna trusted Kai to keep her safe. They were out in deep water in the vastness of the ocean, just him and her and that, in itself, was a mind-blowing experience. She tried not to think about sharks. Kai trod water next to her as she lay on her board, facing the beach.

'The trick is to catch the wave as it curls so it picks you up, then when it breaks it takes your board towards the beach. When you feel the wave lift you, keep your head down, paddle hard and kick if you can so you catch it. Then just hang on tight.'

He made it all sound so easy, but it wasn't and she felt embarrassed at her ineptitude as wave after wave rolled into shore without her. Then finally Kai shouted, 'Now! Paddle, paddle, paddle!' He gave her board a helping hand onto the wave and suddenly she was moving, Kai shouting encouragement. Squealing with exhilaration, she rode the wave into shore, right to where the white waters swirled up onto the sand. 'I did it, I did it! It was so fast, so...so thrilling.'

She looked back to see Kai bodysurfing into shore on the next wave. He got up and made his way through the water towards her, the sun glinting off the droplets of water that clung to his powerful body. With his black hair falling to his shoulders and the bold, dark tattoos on his arm, he looked like some mythical deity emerging from the water that foamed around him. She wanted him so much, she ached.

She wished she had her phone and could take a photo of him. Not that she'd share him with her followers, just her sisters. And only to show them her surfing instructor, not anything personal, not a man she fancied, not a man she had *kissed*. Over the days she'd been here, she'd spent time texting with Eliza and Thea on the group chat as they were on different time zones. Thea was enjoying the snow and had bumped into a familiar face so had a friend to ski with. Eliza was glad the kitesurfing lesson had gone so well and Sienna had thanked her.

'Well-done,' Kai said when he reached her, and briefly hugged her.

She loved his hugs.

'Do that a few more times and once you've got the feel of how to get on a wave, I'll take you out on the surfboard.'

'Then I have to stand up.'

'That's right. You paddle out, pick your wave—I'll pick it for you—catch it and then do your pop up.'

'My pop up?'

'Get into your standing position to ride the wave in. We'll practice on the board on the sand. It's kind of like a push-up only you use your core to jump to your feet as you push.'

'Okay…' she said, realising actual surfing might not be as simple as it sounded.

After several successful rides in on the body-board it was time for her to ride a surfboard proper. Kai laid the large foam board on the sand and showed her how to get up into the standing position, feet parallel on an angle, knees bent, arms out by her sides for balance. Thank heaven for all those hours in the gym.

'You're strong and you're agile,' Kai said approvingly. It must seem like kids' stuff to him, but he was as patient and kind as he had been when teaching her to kitesurf.

'Now I'm going to ride a few waves in,' he said. 'Watch me carefully when I pop up, how I angle myself, how I use my arms to balance.'

For the next twenty minutes Sienna watched, awestruck, as Kai made catching a wave look effortless. He was as one with his board, with the waves—like a dance. Strong and muscular yet graceful as befit a world-class champion. She was so intent on admiring him, she doubted she picked up any tips on surfing technique. It was difficult not to daydream about what a night together at his house might bring.

Then Kai was with her again and it was time for her to try surfing. On a long foam board. Standing up and catching a wave.

She could do it.

The waves seemed bigger than they had been, although Kai assured her they weren't. And it wasn't working for her the way it had with the bodyboard. It seemed impossible to get up and stay up without falling off. She was wiped out several times, tumbled over and over under the water, mouth full of salt, hair waving in front of her face, not sure which way was up. She was tiring and about to give up—after all, the bucket list was about trying surfing, not necessarily succeeding at it. Then Kai was beside her. 'This wave. Now. Paddle, paddle, paddle. You're on. Now get up...*up*. Keep your knees bent. Balance with your arms. Let the wave do the work. You've done it. You're surfing!'

Sienna triumphantly rode the wave into shore, staying upright on the board without too many wobbles until right up to where the white water was knee-deep. Kai bodysurfed in on the wave behind her.

'I...I did it,' she said, dazed with triumph. 'I surfed a wave. I stayed on and I surfed.'

'How did it feel?'

She pushed the wet hair out of her face and turned to look at him. 'Good. Fun. Amazing, in fact.'

'You nailed it. Are you ready to go out again?'

She paused. 'No, I don't want to go out again. I've caught a wave and I'm leaving on a high note.'

He frowned. 'What do you mean?'

She took a deep breath. 'I've now checked off surfing from my bucket list. I'm glad I did it. And I'm so grateful to you for helping me. But I don't think I'm a surfer. It would take a lot of practice to get competent and I didn't like it enough to want to do that. I know it's your sport—your life—and I don't want to disappoint you or offend you. But surfing is not for me.'

'It's good you recognise that so soon.'

'My mother says I know my own mind and I make decisions quickly. I want to be a kite-surfer. When I go back home, I'm going to find a kitesurfing school near London and keep on with it.' She paused. 'I know it won't be the same as in Bora Bora—nothing would be the same anywhere but Bora Bora—but I love it. And I thank you for that too.'

He nodded. 'You have passion. You can't be halfhearted to excel at a sport. I always wanted to surf—my grandmother says I was born with the surf in my veins. I used to sneak away from school to ride waves any chance I could.'

'What did your parents think about that?'

His face tightened. 'They weren't happy. Threatened to send me to boarding school in France.'

'That sounds dramatic,' she said. 'Although if you were surfing Teahupoo they must have been worried sick about your safety.'

'It wasn't that.' He took an abrupt step back. 'I don't want to talk about it.'

'Okay,' she said, surprised at the sudden grimness of his expression. This was a Kai she hadn't seen before.

'You worked hard,' he said. 'You must be hungry. I certainly am. We should head back to the house for lunch.'

Sienna could tell he was forcing his voice to sound normal. There was an undercurrent there that didn't encourage her to ask further questions about his parents. 'Yes, I am hungry, that would be great.'

His shoulders visibly relaxed. 'After lunch I have a treat for you. There's excellent snorkelling on the other side of the *motu*.'

'Snorkelling? That's something else I've learned here that I want to continue.'

'There's a colony of green turtles living in the waters of the bay.'

'I would absolutely love to see a turtle. In fact, nothing could delight me more than to snorkel with turtles.' Well, apart from further kissing— and going further than kissing—with Kai.

'There's a very good chance you'll do that this afternoon.'

'Really? You're rather good at making my dreams come true, aren't you, Kai Hunter?'

CHAPTER EIGHT

EXQUISITE, MULTIHUED MARINE life teemed in the pristine waters of the secluded bay on Motu Puaiti, but to Kai nothing trumped the sight of Sienna in her sleek, black one-piece swimsuit as she glided through the crystal-clear water in pursuit of an elusive turtle. The swimsuit hugged every curve, was sexier even than that bronze bikini. He didn't know her well enough—yet—to suggest that swimming naked here would be the ultimate. But one day...

She took such delight in nature, was so graceful and confident in the water. He thought she would love scuba. Who knew? One day perhaps he could help her check that off her bucket list too. Until this morning—when he had fully kissed her and she had kissed him back—he wouldn't have allowed himself such a thought. Now he let himself think more than a day ahead with Sienna—because it was beginning to seem unbearable that he would have her in his life for only a few more days.

He delighted in his private island, which he had owned for less than a year. His pleasure in his possession was doubled by sharing it with Sienna. Who knew she would feel such a connection to the house?

His strategy for his company had given him everything he wanted in terms of material advantage, but had his strategy for his personal life worked out as well? He realised for all his wealth, for all his avoiding of emotional entanglement, he was lonely. And his current lifestyle didn't allow for him to look after his own child. Although Kinny could not be getting more loving care from his grandparents, it wasn't a situation that could continue.

These past few days since he'd met Sienna had highlighted just how lacking his life was of a deeply personal connection. He felt so relaxed with her, he didn't have to prove anything. Somehow, she got him—like no other woman had. They shared so many interests, could they share a life?

He hadn't been 100 percent truthful when he'd told her he wasn't sure about what he wanted to do with this place—he had purchased it to one day be a home base for him and Kinny. How the logistics of that would work out was still fuzzy. But seeing Sienna taking such delight in the house had brought some of that fuzziness into focus. He could see her living here too. How that could work seemed impossible right now, but Kai hadn't achieved what he had by stamping down on dreams or not making the impossible become possible. However, his best plan here was still to take it day by day with Sienna—or perhaps refine that down to hour by hour.

He swam along the calm surface of the water with her, looking down into a world of colourful corals, stripey fish and the languid pace of a green turtle gliding its way through the water. Sienna dived down for a closer look, but the shy turtle swam in between two rocks and out of sight. Sienna surfaced and removed her snorkel from her mouth.

'I think that handsome turtle has had enough of us humans admiring him. Isn't he gorgeous though? I don't know if it is a *he*. Do you know how to tell whether a turtle is male or female?'

'No idea,' he said. 'Beyond my scope of knowledge.'

'I'll look it up when we get back to the house,' she said.

'Does it matter?'

'I suppose not. I just want to use the correct pronoun.'

'I'm sure the turtle will appreciate that,' he said.

'You're laughing at me.'

'No. I'm amused. I think it's cute that you care.'

'Maybe,' she said with a reluctant smile.

'Definitely,' he said.

They took off their fins and sat together on the warm, wet sand, under the shade of a cluster of palm trees, looking out to the translucent waters of the bay, myriad hues of aquamarine and turquoise and white, white sand, she in her swimsuit, he in board shorts. The water lapped gently against the sand.

She drew her knees up to her chest. 'Three green turtles and a blue starfish. What more could I ask for?'

'And another item checked off your bucket list.'

She turned to him. 'Sorry I didn't take to surfing. I hope you're not disappointed in me.'

'Why would I be disappointed? Surfing is my obsession. That doesn't mean you'll like it. I believe a sport like surfing chooses you, not the other way around.'

'I...I have to confess the waves scared me. It was terrifying to be wiped out. Tumbling around and around, not sure which way was up, swallowing salt water, fearing my board was going to bang me on the head and knock me out. I was so glad you were there to keep me safe.'

'It's wise to have a healthy respect for the

sea,' he said. 'Every wave is different. No two are the same. They can be unpredictable.'

'And dangerous.'

'Yet you're not scared of the swell when you're kitesurfing.'

'It's different. I feel more in control, with my feet secured on the board and the control bar to hold on to. While I know kitesurfers go out in big waves, I can't see myself ever doing that.'

'You could kitesurf in this bay. No surf or strong currents to take you where you could get into trouble.'

'And snorkelling here is like being in some aquatic heaven.'

'I couldn't argue with that.' Having her here with him made it perfect.

She looked up at him, her green eyes wide, her wet hair slicked back off her face, her cheeks flushed. 'This day has been truly memorable.' She took his hand in hers. 'You are the most wonderful, generous man to share this with me. I will never forget this island or you.'

He didn't want her to forget him. He wouldn't *let* her forget him. Something deep, hitherto unmined, shifted behind the barricades he had built up against emotion and urged him to recognise how important she was.

She reached up and kissed him, a sweet, salty kiss, her mouth soft and warm and inviting.

Sienna.

In a moment of profound recognition, he responded to that pleasurable pressure, acknowledged that connection with this special person, before pulling her close. He deepened the kiss using his mouth and tongue, thrilling at the closeness of her body.

At last.

He'd been wanting her all day. Needing her to affirm there was something there between them. Strong. Compelling. So unexpected it was like a gift.

He took it easy with her at first, knowing she had been reticent about him touching her, wondering what the story was behind that reticence. A slight breeze danced over their skin to cool them. He felt a shiver go through her that had nothing to do with the fact they were wet from the sea—no, it was a shiver of anticipation that thrilled him. With a low murmur of need, she kissed him back, matching his urgency, looping her arms around his neck to bring him even closer.

His chest was bare, the fabric of her swimsuit fine and wet and he could feel the curves of her body, the peaking of her nipples against his skin as if there was nothing at all between them. He slid his hands down the smooth skin of her neck, pushing the straps of her swimsuit down so they fell to the tops of her arms. He broke away from her mouth, pressed a trail of small kisses along the hollows of her throat, across her bare shoulders towards the swell of her breasts. She gasped, stilled, pulled back from him and fumbled with her swimsuit straps to pull them back up onto her shoulders. With a deep shudder of unfulfilled need, he let go of her. She couldn't meet his eyes, her lovely mouth trembling and swollen from his kisses.

She had never looked more beautiful.

She took a deep, steadying breath. 'Kai, I'm loving this. I...I want you so much. I really do. I'm sorry. But...I'm...I'm inhibited. On the beach I feel too exposed. Silly really, I know, as we're on a private island and no one is going to come along and discover us. But what if a helicopter or drone flew over?'

He cleared his throat. 'Unlikely, but possible.'

'Truth is. Well. I...I'm new to all this.' Her words blurted out. 'I mean, I've never slept with anyone but my ex.' She turned to stare straight out to sea as she said it, as if embarrassed to admit it. 'I'm thirty-two with the dating experience of an eighteen-year-old. But there it is. I fooled around a bit with my high school boyfriend, but my ex, well, he was my first and uh...only lover. I met him in the first week at university.'

What a fool that guy had been to let her go. Kai didn't know the whole story, he didn't *want* to know the whole story—but he knew she had been deeply unhappy and that it had eroded her confidence in the beautiful, smart, lovable woman she was.

He cupped her chin to turn her back round to see him, willing her to recognise the truth of his gaze. 'Look at me. There's nothing wrong with that,' he said. 'I'm sure you had a horde of guys pursuing you after your divorce.'

'Yes. No. Not really. I wasn't interested, you see. I…couldn't imagine trusting anyone ever again. There was a friend I'd known for a long time, we thought we might try, but there was no chemistry. It didn't happen and—'

'Sienna. I don't need to know your history—'

'Such as it is, when it comes to sex,' she said with a twist to her mouth. Her very kissable mouth. He wanted to kiss her again.

He never wanted to stop kissing her.

'The only thing that matters to me is that we're here together,' he said. 'Nothing else counts. It's just you and me and we want each other. Consenting adults. That's all we need to know.'

'Thank you. You're so nice. Kind.'

And very, very horny.

That black swimsuit was meant to conceal but it clung to her curves, and her nipples were clearly visible. Her mouth was still swollen from his kisses; when she moistened it with the tip of her tongue it nearly drove him crazy with want. Was she as aroused as he was?

But he had to reluctantly agree with her that, for her sake, perhaps the beach in the late afternoon wasn't the best place to make love. Nor might it be the best time—she was still smarting from her divorce; that was obvious. He wanted her to come to him without reservation. He also felt that, as only her second lover, he wanted to make that experience utterly memorable for her. He didn't want to think of her with any other man, but her husband didn't sound like a nice guy, selfish and controlling, hardly the attributes of a good lover. Kai wanted to give Sienna the exciting, fulfilling loving she deserved.

'Do you want to stay here on the bay for a while longer?' he said. 'We could have a final swim. We might not get back here again during your visit to Bora Bora.'

Her mouth turned down. 'I guess I might not, sad though it is to say it. The days go so fast in the rundown to the end of a holiday, don't they?'

He wanted to tell her that her farewell to the island didn't have to mean goodbye to him. They could keep in touch. He was often in Europe. It wouldn't be at all difficult to book in a visit to London. But to what point? They came from different worlds. And he wasn't looking for a casual girlfriend—a fly in, fly out booty call. Not anymore. Not since Kinny came into his life.

A quiet, insistent inner voice nagged at him—*not since Sienna came into my life.*

'You still have a few days,' he said. 'Are there any more bucket list goals I can help you with?'

Her face brightened. 'There is something. Pearls. Black Tahitian pearls are so famous and I can't go home without some. I particularly would like to buy a necklace for my mother. The people I met on the shuttle bus are planning to go to the pearl farm at Rangiroa. They said it was highly recommended.'

'You would enjoy that, I'm sure. Rangiroa is also a good island for scuba and snorkelling—there's a chance you might swim with dolphins. But it is quite a long way from here. The flight is more than two hours or there is a ferry that takes more than five hours. Are you particularly interested in the production process of the pearls or in shopping for pearls?'

'Both.' She paused. 'But I have five days left here and that includes Christmas Day. I don't know that I want to spend the best part of a day getting there and back when I could be kitesurfing or snorkelling.'

'Or spending time with me,' he said.

She looked up at him; her smile was slow and sensual. 'That too.'

'One of my uncles owns a highly regarded jewellery shop in Vaitape. I could take you there. He'd look after you and make sure you got the best quality and the best value pearls. He also has displays that show the way Tahitian pearls are grown.'

'That sounds like an idea,' she said. 'I want the gift I get for Mum to be really special.'

'It sounds like you care for her very much.'

'I do. She is the best possible mother as my father is the best possible father. Three girls must have been a handful at times. We're all very different and with one of us so sick—'

'One of you was sick? Was it you?' Fear struck him at the thought.

'Not me. My younger sister, Eliza.'

'Was it serious?'

'She was diagnosed with acute myeloid leukaemia when she was six. It's a cancer of the blood and bone marrow.'

'That sounds very serious. How old were you then?'

'Thirteen, old enough to be very aware of what was happening to my adored baby sister. Old enough to want to do everything in my power to help her. It came back a second time when she was fourteen. Eliza spent a lot of time in and out of hospital, needing regular medication and checkups.'

Kai saw the concern on her face, the remembered pain and fear for her sister. The family must have lived on the knife edge of losing a beloved daughter and sister for a very long time.

'There were other illnesses too—Eliza's health was a worry to us over many years. We were all very protective of her. I went to university close by so I could be with her if I was needed. She wasn't given the all-clear until she was twenty. It was a big stress on the family, not that we minded, we all pulled together to help in any way we could. If the power of our love could have cured her, she would never have needed chemotherapy.'

'Of course,' he said soberly, thinking of Sienna as a young teenager displaying such compassion.

'We were all affected in some way by the necessity of caring for Eliza. The biggest impact was on my parents, my mother, Lila in particular. She was a teacher in a private school. But when Eliza became ill, Mum took a step back from her job. She filled in on a temporary basis when Eliza's hospital stays and appointments allowed, which pushed her right off the career ladder. Not that she ever complained, but it took a toll on her. She loves pearls and I want to surprise her with some when I see her after Christmas. She deserves it.'

'We'll get the best for your mother. There are various gradings of Tahitian pearls. My uncle will make sure you get the best quality.'

'Thank you. I do need guidance because in the shops all the necklaces and bracelets looked beautiful to me. I wouldn't know what was a good pearl or not.'

Kai paused. 'Am I wrong in thinking your sister's illness has something to do with you being in Bora Bora by yourself for Christmas? You say Christmas is a big deal in your family and yet you and your sisters end up scattered around the world. What about your parents? Where are they?'

'My parents? They decided to celebrate their fortieth wedding anniversary by going on a cruise that took them away from London for Christmas.'

'They didn't invite you?'

She shrugged. 'I guess they didn't want their adult children on their anniversary cruise.'

'Do I detect you weren't happy about that?'

'Of course I was happy for them. Well… maybe I wondered why they had to be away on Christmas Day when we've *always* celebrated Christmas together as a family. Maybe I had to fight a few hurt feelings. But they had gone through a lot. There was the strain of taking care of Eliza for all those years and worrying about the effect of it on me and Thea, too, most likely. They probably need time to be a couple again, maybe to plan their future. It's difficult for adult kids to see their parents as individuals with their own hopes and dreams, isn't it?'

Kai thought for a moment before answering her. He didn't like to talk about his family. But he felt he needed to tell Sienna about the circumstances that had shaped him. And her warm acceptance made it so much easier to talk about things he would prefer to stay buried. 'In my case, I had parents who couldn't see their youngest son's hopes and dreams and were determined to smash them and impose their hopes on me.'

She frowned. 'Which were?'

'Let me give you some background.'

'I'd like that very much.' She seemed genuinely interested and he appreciated that. This wasn't easy.

He was notorious for keeping his private life private. Yet, Kai found himself wanting to open up to Sienna. 'My parents are both smart, ambitious people who come from established, well-off families, in my father's case a French family. My mother has a high-ranking role in government administration. My father is a lawyer in his family firm. Status is important to them.'

'A touch on the stuffy side, then.'

He laughed. 'You could say that.'

'Do you have brothers and sisters?'

'I'm the youngest of three brothers. My older brother is a lawyer—now in the family firm— the middle brother is a doctor. They both went to university in France—and that was expected of me too.'

'France. That's a long way to go to university from here.'

'And too far from some of the best surf in the world,' he reminded her, and she smiled. 'The relative merits of surf breaks meant absolutely nothing to my parents.'

'I can see that. What did they plan for you?'

'They pegged me as an engineer, because I was good at making things with my hands. I didn't want to be an engineer or any career that required years of study. School was a struggle for me, I'll admit it. Why the private school never picked up I was dyslexic I don't know. All I knew was the more they berated me for being lazy and a troublemaker, and nothing like my studious brothers, the more I rebelled.'

'So you started missing school to go surfing?'

'Whenever I could. Surfing was my escape and I was good at it. Really good. I was winning junior championships. I was a sportsman. I looked out for adventure. If that meant crewing on a yacht for a few days, I took off without telling anyone who might have stopped me. I missed so much school, I failed my exams and was expelled at age sixteen. Much to my parents' disgust and disappointment. To them I was a waste of space.'

Sienna slowly shook her head. 'I…I don't know what to say. It seems very unreasonable of them. Weren't they pleased at how you were excelling with surfing?'

'Surfing didn't count to them as a sport like tennis or rugby.'

'But surfing is an Olympic sport now.'

'I know but it wasn't then. Surfing didn't rate.'

Her eyes narrowed. 'Were either of them brave enough to surf Teahupoo?'

'Of course not,' he said.

'There we go, then,' she said, and he liked the way she was sticking up for him.

'I was a disappointment in every way. They washed their hands of me.'

'You were only sixteen.' Her lovely face was creased in sympathy. 'I'm so sorry to hear that. It's difficult for me to understand, as my parents have always been so accepting and loving to me and my sisters.'

'You were lucky. My brothers were lucky they did what was expected of them. I was sixteen and on the cusp of a surfing career. But that meant nothing to my parents. I didn't follow the path they set out for me. The path I'd chosen for myself simply wasn't acceptable.'

'It must have been really uncomfortable for you to stay at home.'

'I couldn't stay. Fortunately for me, my grandparents believed in me and took me into their home on Bora Bora.'

'The same grandparents that own my resort?'

'The same wonderful people, my mother's parents. Of course they disapproved of how my parents treated me but couldn't say anything in the interests of family diplomacy.'

'Seems to me that their actions spoke for them.'

'They did. They gave me a home on their private island with them, supported my surfing in every way. When I wasn't away surfing, I was working in the resort helping them and I learned a lot about business and how everything works.'

'What about your brothers? I can't imagine my sisters letting me go too easily.'

'We're good, they're on my side. I think they're proud I've made my own way.'

'How awful to have to take sides in a family.'

He shrugged. 'That's the way it is. My middle

brother Armand married a French woman he met at university there and they live in Lyons. The teenagers you saw on the kite boards are their daughters back here for Christmas.'

'And the other brother?'

'Jules lives in Papeete near my parents. He married a girl he knew from school in Papeete, and works with my father at the family law firm. He followed exactly the path they set out for him, but I doubt he would force his son to do the same. He invested in my company. As did my grandparents. They gave me the money I needed when I started Wave Hunters.'

Sienna frowned. 'I'm sorry, I don't want to criticise your parents but how could your mother, in particular, abandon you like that?'

He shrugged. 'She is, as you say in English, 'under the thumb' of my father. He's not to be crossed.'

'Yet you crossed him.'

'I did, and don't regret it. My mother used to meet me behind his back on the pretext of visiting my grandparents, on Bora Bora. But she could never be open about it.'

'Surely he knew?'

He shrugged again. 'Who knows? But his pride would never let him admit he knew about it because that would be condoning my "bad" behaviour.'

'Your grandparents are the heroes of the day. I hope I bump into them at the resort.'

'They recognised my talent and that perhaps I should be allowed to follow my own dreams—not those that had been set out for me by others.'

'And how it paid off for you—and the people who believed in you.'

All true. And yet everyone in his family was happily married. He had resisted it all the way. Even his beloved child had come to him without any effort on his part. He might be a billionaire, but he was a pauper when it came to emotional fulfilment. And at the age of thirty-five, he was beginning to realise what he might have missed.

CHAPTER NINE

SIENNA ALMOST DREADED the sun going down as it would mark the end of this magical day with Kai. But there was still light in the sky as this part of the world headed for the solstice, the longest day. And the promise of the evening spent in the privacy of Kai's superb house might be an even more exciting end to the day.

He turned to her. His face was very serious, and her heart turned over at how handsome he was and how familiar he had become.

How much she wanted him.

'Thank you for listening to me. Not many people know about my history with my family.'

'I'm honoured you shared it with me.'

He dropped a light kiss on her mouth. Even that brief touch sent shivers of pleasure through her. 'Thank you. That means something coming from you with your perfect family.'

'I never said it was perfect. There were stresses. We've all had our squabbles and disagreements. But we're not cruel and we don't hold grudges.

So yeah, maybe my family is kinda perfect.' She had to stop herself from tearing up at the thought of how much she missed her family. But would she honestly swap this time with Kai in Bora Bora to be back in Chiswick?

'You're lucky,' he said.

'Yes,' she said. She wouldn't have got through the horrible marriage breakup without her family, that was for sure. 'What is your relationship like with your parents now?'

'Uneasy might be the best way to put it.'

'Surely you proved your own path was the right path for you with the success of Wave Hunters? Have they not acknowledged that?'

'Grudging respect might be the way to describe their attitude to me now. Money talks,' he said with a bitter twist to his mouth.

'So no reconciliation?'

He shook his head. 'Tentative. Thanks to the efforts of my grandparents. Some ground has been broken. This year they've invited all the family to their home on their *motu* for Christmas Day.'

'How lovely,' Sienna said, thinking wistfully of the house in Chiswick standing forlorn this year with not even a Christmas wreath on the front door. Families all over these islands would be celebrating Christmas together while she would be on her own at the resort. Even the older couple she'd met on the shuttle was going home for Christmas. There would be no point in her doing that—because this year for the first time there was no family Christmas. These past few days with Kai had put that gloomy prospect to the back of her mind but now it came rushing forward.

'I noticed there were a lot of Christmas decorations in town when I was there yesterday. Christmas seems to be as big a celebration here as it is back home. Doesn't a Christmas gathering usually happen each year with your family?'

'When we were little, yes. But once we went our own ways, we didn't always spend Christmas together. Sometimes my parents visit Armand and his family in France. Sometimes I'm on the other side of the world. However, I try to get back here for my grandparents' sake although sometimes it's inconvenient and I'd rather not. To be honest, Christmas doesn't hold a lot of happy memories for me.'

'Why is this year special?'

He paused, to Sienna it seemed an uncomfortable pause and she wondered why. 'Because the great-granddaughters are here.'

'I see,' she said. Of course. Children. That was what Christmas was all about. She had dreamed of her own babies enjoying the wonder of a Kendall family Christmas. Each year the longing had grown stronger.

'The adults will make an effort to tolerate each other,' Kai said with a wry twist to his mouth.

'I hope you do try and keep the peace for the children's sakes. Christmas is such a special time.' And a special time to learn to be independent, she told herself sternly.

'Talking of Christmas…is there any other bucket list item you'd like me to help you with before then?' he said.

Sienna nodded slowly.

She wouldn't share the mind-blowing sex one.

'Yes, there is. It might sound silly, but I've always had a yearning to sleep under the stars. I don't know where I got that fanciful wish from, but it's always been there. Maybe from reading too many children's adventure books.'

'I've slept under the stars many times. It's a beautiful experience and an aim worthy of a bucket list.'

'I'm glad you think so too. I've never had the chance to do it. London has too much light pollution. Then when I've been out in the country it's been too cloudy or wet, or I've been with other people who weren't interested.' Callum, of course, but she didn't want to bring him into this conversation in any way.

'You're in just the right place to easily check that goal off. The night sky on this island is magnificent.'

'You mean here? Tonight?' she said.

'We could sleep on the beach.'

We. There it was again and she liked it.

'You would be with me?'

'Of course,' he said. 'If anything, I'll have to protect you from the giant mosquitoes that will try to carry you away from me.' He laughed. 'Seriously, the mosquitoes might be a problem.'

'Surely not if we spray on the tropical strength insect repellent? I have some in my bag.'

'There's more in the house.'

'We'll just spray ourselves, then.'

'I don't believe there's a tent in that store-room, but there are some beach shelters. This is our wet season and at this time of the year there could be showers throughout the night. We don't want to get caught in them.'

'A beach shelter sounds good. So long as at some stage I can lie on my back and look up at the star-filled skies and just...well, just take it all in.'

'Will you make a wish?' he said.

'A wish? I hadn't thought of making a wish upon a star. But now you've mentioned it, I shall. And you?'

'I'll think about my wish,' he said. 'Who knows? Maybe we're only ever permitted one wish upon one star so I had better make it worthwhile.'

She frowned. 'I didn't know you could only

have a once-ever wish on a star. I mean, there are so many stars and so many nights.'

He was obviously trying to stop himself from laughing. 'I don't know that either. But it makes sense for a very special wish, doesn't it? I mean, if you can have a good-luck wetsuit…?'

'You're teasing me!'

'Am I?' he said with a quirk of a black eyebrow.

She laughed. 'Yes, you are.'

And she liked it.

He got up from the sand, held his hand out to her. 'Come on. How about a final snorkel around the bay before we go up to the house and plan the night expedition.'

'You know, I'd really like just a swim, a lovely, leisurely swim in the most beautiful water in the world. The snorkelling was so perfect earlier I don't want to risk that it won't be as wonderful again, if you know what I mean.'

'Whatever you'd like to do is fine by me,' he said.

Her own wishes had become less and less important during her marriage as she became subsumed by another person—this holiday was all about taking charge of her own life again, doing what she wished to do instead of what someone else wanted to do.

But how much better everything seemed simply by being with Kai.

'I'll race you into the water,' she said.

* * *

She and Kai were both hungry after all the swimming and snorkelling. There'd been kissing, too, both laughing about their new skills in kissing in the water. She appreciated the way he didn't pressure her to go further until she was ready and sure of her privacy.

Back at the house, she helped him put together an early dinner from preprepared meals left early that morning by the housekeeper. It felt quite startlingly domestic—and she liked the intimacy of it.

He was adept in the kitchen. 'After competing on the surfing circuit, at beaches all around the world and sometimes in the most remote places, I can prepare food anywhere,' he explained.

She was wearing her new *pareo*, in colourful splashes of orange, yellow and white, tied around the neck in a halter style, which added to the informal atmosphere. Kai, too, wore a *pareo*, dark green, slung low around his hips. She gasped when she first saw him in it.

'I don't know if that means you like me in a *pareo* or you're shocked by me wearing a skirt,' he said with a laugh.

'I...I like,' she had to choke out. 'I like very much.' In fact, she liked it so much that if she were a different person, bolder, more experienced perhaps, she would tell him to skip the dinner, take him by the hand and drag him straight to the bedroom. Or maybe the sofa; it was closer. Did he wear underwear or was a *pareo* like a Scotsman's kilt?

'It's traditional wear for men in our culture,' he said. 'And very practical for the climate.'

'You look very, very good in it,' she said, her voice a little choked by how much she wanted him.

'Not as good as you look in yours,' he said as he made a slow inspection of the way her *pareo* was wrapped around her body.

In truth, once she'd seen Kai in his *pareo*, her appetite for food was overwhelmed by her appetite for him. But she joined him in the meal. They feasted on local specialities *poisson cru*, raw tuna marinated in lime juice and coconut juice and mixed with vegetables, and *poulet fafa*, a spicy chicken baked in taro leaves, plus salads and fresh fruit.

'It's like dining in a restaurant,' Sienna said. 'Only it has the feel of a picnic.'

'Our family has exacting standards when it comes to food. Healthy food is important, and it has to taste great too. We have a wonderful heritage here of our original Polynesian food and French cuisine the colonists brought with them.'

'I've enjoyed every meal I've had since I've been here,' she said.

But none as much as this one with just him and her alone together in a beautiful house on a private tropical island. 'Please thank your house-keeper,' she said. 'There's a lot of food. Did your housekeeper know you had a visitor?'

'I told her, yes. But don't be surprised if curious eyes saw us taking off from Mareva in the speedboat.'

'Is it... Is it usual for you to spend time with the guests?'

'No. That is why those curious eyes find it notable that I have spent time with you.' He looked into her eyes. 'One time I got involved with a guest—never again.'

'Oh,' she said, not sure she wanted to hear about it.

'You want to know, don't you?'

'Only if you want to tell me,' she said. She couldn't expect him not to be experienced—in fact, that could be an advantage considering her history—but she didn't like the idea of him with another woman, although she had no claim on him.

'I was eighteen, she was an older woman. Well, she seemed much older to me but she was probably in her thirties.'

'That's too old for an eighteen-year-old.'

'I didn't think so at the time. Cut a long story short, she seduced me. I went willingly. I was infatuated with her. I didn't know she was married. She was toying with me. I was devastated when she left the island without saying goodbye.'

She could imagine how beautiful Kai must have been as an eighteen-year-old boy, irresistible, perhaps to a certain type of woman. She remembered back when she was eighteen and how naive she'd been, although she'd thought she was so grown-up. Her mother had told her she was too young to settle down with the one boy. She should have listened. Or cut out of the marriage long before she had. In the last years, Callum had started to pull away. He'd worked long hours in his family's property development business, travelling the world in search of new development opportunities and, she'd only belatedly realised, feminine company. Those last years had been totally wasted staying married to him.

'How cruel of that woman to treat you like that,' she said.

'Yeah, it hurt,' Kai said. 'I can't imagine where I thought such a relationship could go but I didn't think she'd just have her fun and move on. I was much more wary in the future. And I never got involved with another guest again. Until now.'

'Until now,' she echoed. 'Why me?'

'Because you're you,' he said simply, and she wasn't sure what to make of that.

Their conversation over the meal flowed easily. Yet Sienna felt a touch stilted, aware that those kisses on the beach had taken them across a divide.

Now she was no longer on a beach in broad daylight where she would be self-conscious about being seen. She wanted him, she knew they were building towards intimacy, yet she sensed a reticence from Kai. If she'd said yes on the beach, she was sure he wouldn't have hesitated to go further than kisses. But now he was, it seemed, studiously not touching her.

Her first thought was, *What have I done?* But that was how Callum had had her thinking, that anything that had gone amiss was her fault. She had done nothing wrong this evening. Neither had Kai. They were still very much getting to know each other.

After dinner they took cool drinks out to an enclosed veranda, with the glass doors and windows open to evening breezes but covered with insect screens. They sat on two vintage cane chaise longues piled with palm-print fabric cushions. The vague hint of mothballs was overwhelmed by the heady scents of rich tropical flowers—gardenia, frangipani, ginger—that wafted into the room.

'I'd suggest we sleep out here, but you wouldn't be directly under the stars and that's not what you want for your bucket list,' he said.

'It has to be right under the stars,' she said. 'I want to feel as if I can reach up and touch them.'

'Then the beach cabana on the sand it will be.' He pointed through the window. 'Look, we've been blessed with a perfect crescent moon in an ink-dark sky, lit with a multitude of stars.'

'Perfect,' she breathed.

'I'll get a cabana from the storeroom. But first there's something I need to tell you.'

Sienna sensed the serious edge to his voice with a sickening dread. Everything had been too perfect. 'Sure,' she said, hoping her voice didn't sound shaky.

'The final revelation from me,' he said.

He was married. Engaged. Otherwise spoken for.

'Fire away,' she said, trying to sound cool and detached.

He moved closer to her, took her hand. 'Sienna, I have a daughter. A little girl, eighteen months old named Kinny, short for Kinepela, which means wave. Her mother chose the name, I did not, but I like it very much and it suits her.'

Sienna caught her breath. 'The little girl on the beach, in the pink swimsuit, that first day I saw you kitesurfing with your nieces. She's your daughter?' Hadn't she suspected it from the start? The bond between them had seemed so strong.

What did this mean for her?

Now it wasn't just Kai, but Kai and a child. Kai and an ex-wife perhaps? It became a different equation.

He nodded. 'I didn't know she existed until a year ago, had no idea I was a father. Kinny was left in a basket at the reception desk at Mareva. There was a note from her mother and a birth certificate naming me as her father.'

Sienna was so shocked she momentarily lost her voice and had to clear her throat to speak. 'You mean a woman abandoned her young baby in a hotel lobby in Bora Bora?' She, who longed for a baby of her own, couldn't comprehend how another woman could give hers away.

He nodded.

'And she wasn't your wife or your girlfriend, yet she said the baby was yours?'

'That's right. I recognised the name, of course. She was a woman named Paige. I'd met her at a surfing event in Sri Lanka. Paige was the physiotherapist to the Australian surf team. We hung out, I liked her a lot, but she kept me at arm's length.'

Good, Sienna thought.

She was distinctly uncomfortable at the thought

of Kai with another woman. In fact, jealousy snaked through her, burning and fierce. Even though she had no right to feel that way.

Kai continued. 'Until the last night we were there. We spent the night together, but she made it very clear that it was only to be that one night and she didn't want to see me another time, or keep in touch. She was gone in the morning and I didn't see her again.'

'And then a baby was abandoned at your grandparents' resort? The poor little thing, was she okay?'

'In perfect health, and doted on by everyone around her ever since.'

'Thank heaven. She looked adorable on the beach. Did anyone meet the mother, Paige?'

'No one. But the hotel staff did report a very thin, nervous young woman hovering anxiously around the lobby. By the time the basket was found, she was gone.'

Sienna let go of his hand to take a drink from her glass. 'The poor woman—Paige, I mean. She must have been desperate to leave her baby like that. I cannot imagine anyone would do such a thing lightly.'

'Yes.'

'Are you sure the baby is yours?'

'She looks like me.'

'Is that enough?'

'I had a DNA test to be sure. She is biologically my daughter.'

'How did you feel about suddenly having a daughter? It must have been such a shock.'

How did *she* feel about Kai having a child? It somehow changed the scenario of holiday romance to something else altogether. Her mind raced. If—and it was a big *if*—she and Kai ended up in some kind of ongoing relationship, how would a baby change things? Was he looking for a mother for his child? Or did he not want another woman's influence on her? How would she herself feel about mothering another woman's child?

Kai got up from his chaise longue, paced the length of the veranda and back. 'I didn't know how to feel. It was so unexpected, so sudden. Having kids hadn't been a consideration for me. Suddenly, at age thirty-three, I had an instant family. I didn't know what to do. For the first few days I was a mess. How could I be a father? My apartment in Los Angeles isn't kid friendly. I couldn't take a baby with me when I travelled the world on Wave Hunters business. I don't often come back here because the family situation is so uncomfortable. My grandparents wanted to take her. They even said they would legally adopt her. But that didn't seem right, either.'

'That was quite a dilemma.'

'After a few weeks, Kinny solved all that for me.'

'What do you mean?'

Kai sat down opposite her again. 'I fell in love with her—quite simply, head over heels in love with my then six-month-old daughter. Fiercely, protectively in love. She's my child and the most enchanting little person.' A big smile spread over his face. It warmed Sienna's heart. That could only be a good thing as far as she was concerned, as far as any possible involvement with little Kinny.

'So you're a proud dad.'

'Sadly, still only a part-time dad as I can't run Wave Hunters from here and I can't take her with me on planes to different countries every few weeks. She's happy with my grandparents right now, but that's not how I want it to be for the future. And I'm still learning to be a father.' Would the grandparents give the baby up if they'd wanted to adopt her? Would they make it difficult for any woman serious about Kai?

'Seems to me you're already a father, a good one and a loving one. Kinny sounds adorable.' She paused. This might be asking too much—after all, she was flying out on Boxing Day. 'I…I wish I could meet her.'

'I'd like you to meet Kinny. I had to tell you

about her because I want to invite you to my family's Christmas Day celebration.'

Sienna stared at him. 'You're inviting me for Christmas?'

'As I mentioned earlier, it's special this year because the three great-granddaughters will be together for the first time.'

He hadn't mentioned there were *three* great-granddaughters. She was glad she now knew about Kinny.

'Does your other brother have children?'

'One studious teenage boy who is the apple of my father's eye. He's a good kid.'

'Fitting into the family mould, it seems. Will he be at your grandparents' house for Christmas?'

'I hope so. It will be the first Christmas Kinny will really know what's going on and my *mama'u* and *papa'u* want to make a fuss. They've invited everyone to be there.'

'Everyone? Don't tell me—I think I can guess—your parents haven't been accepting of Kinny and the way she came into your life?'

Kai's eyes clouded. 'My father hasn't even met her. He doesn't acknowledge her because of the way she was born. Another reason to disapprove of me too, of course, for my 'irresponsible' behaviour. Just as he was beginning to accept my success in business. However, for the first time I can remember my mother has stood up to him. She sees Kinny whenever she can and spoils her like she says only a *grandmère* can do. I don't know how anyone can't fall in love with my little daughter, but then I'm biased.'

'Of course you are,' she said, leaning over to kiss him. This man had seemed perfect before, but now this level of love for his daughter made her like and admire him even more. Even if his role as a father meant she might have no chance of a future with him.

'What about Paige? Might Kinny's mother come back to claim her one day?'

Kai sighed. 'Sadly not. In her note she left with Kinny, Paige told me her parents had died long ago, she was an only child and there was no one who would love Kinny when Paige herself could no longer care for her. The baby had to be with her father.'

'*Could no longer care for her*? What…what did that mean? It doesn't sound like anything good.'

'Paige was diagnosed with a particularly virulent form of breast cancer when she was in the early stages of pregnancy with Kinny. She couldn't have treatment while she was pregnant but she chose to go ahead with the pregnancy. She brought Kinny to me when she knew she was dying.'

'Oh, no, Kai. That's tragic. I can't bear to think

of what she must have gone through.' She had to blink back a tear. 'Poor Paige. Poor Kinny.'

'Paige didn't want me to find her, but I managed to track her down to a hospice in Sydney and flew to see her. I was in time to hold her hand and reassure her that Kinny would have all the love she could possibly wish for her, and every advantage money could buy. She died a few days later.'

'Such a tragedy.' Sienna's heart ached for Kinny's mother. She couldn't begin to imagine the pain of knowing she would have to leave her baby.

'Of course I wondered if there was anything I could have done to help her if she'd got in touch earlier. Apparently not.' He paused and Sienna saw the regret on his face, not that he wanted to be with Paige, but that he'd been unable to help the mother of his child. 'Paige was a good person. And a good mother.'

'She certainly sounds like it. Why didn't she tell you about Kinny earlier? When she got pregnant?'

'She said she could never be in love with me—that wounded, as I really liked her—there was no chance of a relationship, and she was frightened I might try to take her baby from her. Apparently, she was convinced she would get the right treatment and survive after Kinny's birth.'

'That's unutterably sad.'

'Yes.'

'You're a good person too. Kinny has good parents.'

'But now only one parent, and I have to learn to be both parents to her.' Would he want a mother for Kinny? Might she be that mother? She reined in her thoughts; she hadn't even met his daughter yet.

'That can't be easy.'

'But it's not a chore—you don't realise until you have a child how much you'll love them.'

'I guess not,' Sienna said, fighting to keep the sadness and longing for a child of her own from her voice. Could she—hypothetically speaking of course, love a child who wasn't her own?

'So will you come to Christmas Day with my family?' said Kai.

'I would love to.'

'In that case you're also invited to breakfast tomorrow with my grandparents so you can meet them and Kinny.'

'Meet Kinny? Tomorrow?' Her heart thudded wildly. 'Do they know they're going to meet me?'

'They will know when I tell them in the morning. And they will make you very welcome.'

CHAPTER TEN

TO SLEEP UNDER the stars. Kai loved how Sienna's bucket list was all about being in nature. How she rejoiced over the sighting of a turtle, whereas some of the women he'd met were far more interested in diamond bracelets or designer clothes as their ultimate wishes.

He had never asked her how she felt about children, but her reactions to his story about finding Kinny told him all he needed to know. If he was to have any kind of continued relationship with Sienna, Kinny would be part of it. He and Kinny came as a package deal.

He went back into the kitchen to get them both another cold drink and take it out onto the veranda. Even with the ceiling fans slowly rotating and the breeze coming through the windows, it was still very warm. He sat down next to Sienna, on her chaise longue, facing her.

'Are you sure your grandparents will want me at the breakfast?' she said with a worried frown.

'Absolutely sure. Our times together on the water, kitesurfing and snorkelling, have been noted. My grandmother, in particular, will want to meet the beautiful English woman who has been taking up so much of my time over the last few days. Not only do I want you to meet Kinny, who is such an important part of my life, but also my *mama'u*.'

Automatically, Sienna put her hand up to her hair, which had dried in a wavy mass as there wasn't a hairdryer at the house and the air was so humid. 'But my hair, my clothes. I didn't expect...'

'Your shorts and pineapple T-shirt will look perfectly fine for breakfast. I'll be wearing shorts too. And your hair is lovely the way it is.'

'If you're sure...'

'I'm very sure. You're a natural beauty.'

'Thank you,' she said with that luminous smile he had come to like so much. 'I'll take that compliment.'

'Talking of clothes,' he said. 'I also want to talk about gift wrapping.'

'Gift wrapping?'

'Gift unwrapping, more to the point.'

Kai smiled at her puzzled expression. He put his hands behind her neck to where she'd tied the ends of the *pareo* in a knot. 'All evening you've been tantalising me with something—

someone—I want very much, all wrapped up in this *pareo*, like a beautiful gift.' He undid the knot and the *pareo* slid to the top of her breasts.

She smiled, a slow smile as she looked directly into his eyes. 'I like being unwrapped, the feel of your hands on my skin, the fabric sliding off my shoulders.' She narrowed her eyes in sensual bliss, which sent his arousal levels rocketing. He kissed her and she kissed him back for a long time until kissing was no longer enough.

He broke away from the kiss. 'Every time you've taken a step this evening, the fabric has slid open to reveal your thighs, leading me to wonder if you're wearing panties.'

'Has it?' Her voice was low and husky. 'Perhaps you need to find out. Isn't the whole point of gift wrapping for it to be removed to reveal the gift beneath?'

'Half the fun is in the unwrapping,' he said hoarsely. Who knew she could be such a sexy tease?

He gently pushed the fabric so it slid apart to reveal her breasts. They were perfect, no more than a handful each, firm and round, with small, pink nipples. He dipped his head to kiss each nipple in turn as they peaked and hardened. She moaned her appreciation and arched towards him.

He tugged the *pareo* so it fell and pooled at

her waist. He pushed it farther to reveal the top of a lacy thong. 'So you are wearing—'

'I'm not really the no-panties type, except when they need to come off.'

'And these need to come off?'

'Yes, please.'

He lowered her back against the chaise, a pillow under her head. 'You know how much I want you?'

'It couldn't be more than how much I want you,' she said. 'All I can think about is how much I want you. I've thought about it all day, ever since— *Oh!*'

She didn't take her gaze off him, her breath becoming ragged, as he slid his hands down her waist to reach the sides of her panties and then down to the tops of her thighs. He pushed the lace aside to slide his fingers to her most sensitive place. She gasped, and he could feel how aroused she was already. He caressed her some more, learning from the murmurs of pleasure deep in her throat, the way she angled her hips towards him, what she liked. He tugged the panties all the way down her legs; she nearly tangled them in her feet in her eagerness to help him get them off.

Then she was naked. She was perfect. He could hardly believe she was here with him, her beautiful body his to claim. This wonderful

woman. He wanted her so much it was agony
to hold back. But he had to put a brake on his
own satisfaction while he made sure of hers.
She raised her hips to make it easier for him
to caress her, but instead he went down on her
and kissed her. He used his lips and tongue to
bring her to a peak of arousal for as long as she
seemed to need it, and then felt her shudder and
cry out his name as she came.

Her face was flushed, her hair damp around
her face, her eyes glittering. Gradually, her
breathing returned to normal. She sat up, put
her hand on his arm. 'Thank you,' she murmured, 'but I thought I was giving you a gift.'

'You did,' he said. 'Your pleasure is my gift.'

'In that case, is there a gift for me to unwrap,
too? I like the way you tie your *pareo* around
your hips. Is it a difficult knot to undo?'

'Not at all. But what you find won't be a surprise,' he said hoarsely.

'But I think I know exactly what to do with
it,' she murmured. 'Please let me return the favour.'

She did, but it felt so good he knew he had
to stop her, before he couldn't stop. He wanted
to come with her, in her. 'Protection,' he said.
'I have to get it from the bedroom.'

'Be quick,' she murmured.

'Don't go away,' he said. They both laughed

as they wondered where she'd go to on a very small island in the middle of the Pacific Ocean.

'I'll be waiting for you,' she breathed. 'And wanting you.'

When he got back just minutes later, she was lying seductively on the chaise longue, beautifully naked. She pulled his head down to hers for a kiss. 'Now. I want you inside me now. I'm ready, Kai, I feel like I've been waiting for you for a very long time.'

Sienna awoke on the chaise longue to Kai gently stroking her face. 'Time to wake up if you want to spend the rest of the night under the stars,' he said.

'I must have fallen asleep,' she said, stifling a yawn as she stretched out. That was what multiple orgasms did for you. She looked up to see his expression, tender and caring, and she remembered their glorious lovemaking, the way he had taken her to heights she had never before soared to. She reached up to kiss him. 'Did I tell you how wonderful you are?'

'Several times,' he said. 'And I told you how wonderful you are.'

'We're wonderful together,' she said.

She felt vaguely hysterical, high on utter sexual satisfaction. She was naked, but felt totally unselfconscious with him. There wasn't an inch of each other's bodies they hadn't explored. His *pareo* was back on, slung low on his hips—the sexiest garment a man could wear. A man with a body like Kai's, that is.

'Yes,' he said, and he only needed to say that one word to affirm everything that had happened between them. 'You'll think I'm even more wonderful when I tell you your bed under the stars is waiting for you.'

She sat up, swung her legs over the side of the chaise. 'What? Where?'

'While you were sleeping, I took the cabana down to the beach, chose a spot with uninterrupted sky views and set it up for us. I also took some flat pillows from the loungers to put on the sand as you might find it scratchy to sleep on.'

'You've thought of everything,' she said slowly. Just for her. She'd been married all those years and this man cared for her needs more in a matter of days that her ex ever had.

'Including this.' Kai held up a spray can of mosquito repellent.

'That's not very romantic,' she said, screwing up her nose.

'There's nothing romantic about being bitten all over by mosquitoes.'

'I guess not,' she sighed.

Sienna stood still while he sprayed her. Then did the same for him, feeling possessive about his magnificent body. *Hers, all hers.* She welcomed any opportunity to touch him. She ran her fingers along the tattoos on his upper left arm. 'Do I spray it on your tattoos?'

'Yes,' he said, obviously amused. 'They're just ink on skin.'

'They're really distinctive tattoos. I notice a lot of people have them here.'

'They're part of our culture. The early missionaries banned them—and made both men and women wear clothes.'

'That was a shame. On both counts.'

'We reclaimed both our tattoos and our *pareos*,' he said. 'The tattoos are unique to each person and usually tell a story.'

'What do yours tell?'

'Of my connection to the sea and my reverence for its power.'

'That makes absolute sense,' she said.

He tucked her *pareo* around her, even the slightest grazing of his fingers seemed like a caress to her highly sensitised body, and she followed him outside.

He turned off the outside lights so there were none on at the house. He handed her a torch. 'You'll get used to the light of the moon and the stars, but at first it will seem very dark.'

Making her way down to the beach by torchlight with Kai seemed like something out of a beautiful dream. Their two torch beams danced across the blue-and-white-striped beach cabana. It was set well back from the waves, and two long, flat cushions taken from the loungers were spread out in front of it. 'The cabana is only there in case it rains during the night. We don't need to get under it now or it will hinder your view.'

'The sky is even better than I imagined,' she said, looking up.

'Let's lie down on the cushions and switch off the torches. You'll get the full impact then.'

Immediately, they were plunged into absolute darkness. Sienna lay next to Kai, his arm around her, her head nestled on his shoulder, as she looked up to the vast velvet canopy of the sky—the crescent moon, the multitude of glittering stars. She wriggled her toes in the gritty coral sand to ground her. Gradually, her eyes became accustomed to the darkness and she realised the new moon and the stars gave off their own faint, silvery light. 'There are so many stars I feel lost in them. What an amazing feeling,' she whispered.

'There's no need to whisper. There's no one to hear us.'

'It seems somehow more respectful to whisper,' she whispered.

She could hear the smile in his voice. 'Then whisper...'

The only other sounds were the soft roar of the waves surging onto the sand, then swishing back down to the sea, the rustle of palm leaves picking up a breeze, the sound of birds resettling themselves in the leaves of the tropical shrubs, their own breathing.

'I have to pinch myself to prove this is all real,' she whispered. She twisted to kiss him. 'You smell of mosquito repellent.'

'So do you, but I don't care,' he said, kissing her back.

She started. 'I saw a shooting star!'

'Did you make a wish?'

'I was too late.'

'Keep watching. There'll be others.'

She scarcely dared blink her eyes in case she missed the next shooting star. When another streaked across the sky she wished—she wished so hard she could feel every dream and hope she'd ever suppressed through all those years of her dreadful marriage banging against the barriers she'd erected, clamouring to be set free. But this wish was very much from her here and now.

I wish upon a star for a second chance to live my dreams.

She didn't want this time with Kai to end. She was greedy for more time with him to see if this thing between them could become something real and not just a holiday fantasy.

'Did you wish?' she whispered.

'Yes.'

'I did too. What did you wish?'

'You know I can't tell you or it won't come true. I don't intend to ask you what you wished.'

'Okay. I won't ask. Let's keep our wishes secret.'

What did he wish for?

She looked up at the sky again for a long time, mesmerised by the hundreds and thousands of stars. There was another shooting star and she dared venture another wish.

Let that second chance be with Kai, no matter how impossible it seems.

'Kai? Are you awake?' She thought he might have drowsed off.

'Yes.'

'Thank you for this, for everything. It's exceeded my wildest fantasies of what sleeping under the stars would be like. It's perfect.'

'I'm glad.'

'But it could be even more perfect.'

'What would make it even more perfect?'

'If we made love under the stars.'

She turned into him. Her *pareo* had slid off, and she undid Kai's so she could press her naked body against his, revel in his hard muscles, the satin smoothness of his skin, thrill to the insistence of his erection. They made love slowly, leisurely, to finally reach a mutual release, and then another, as their cries mingled in the stillness of the night. They were so in tune with each other's needs it was as if they had made love many times before.

After Kai fell asleep with her wrapped in his arms, Sienna stayed awake for a long time, replete with sensual satisfaction, looking up at the sky. Drowsily, she wondered if someone with a powerful telescope had ever counted every single one of those stars. She tried to force her eyes to stay open; she wanted this time to go on forever. If she wished hard enough the special, special night would never end.

She awoke several hours later with warm tropical rain splashing on her. She wanted to stay out under the rain and get wet but Kai convinced her she should get under the shelter of the cabana. It wouldn't be easy to get back to sleep while they were drenched and they'd have to go back to the house, he'd said. She didn't want that—this was to be an entire night spent under the stars. Only that would fulfil her bucket wish.

He was right, of course. There was a certain pleasure in sitting dry under the shelter of the cabana, leaning back against Kai's solid chest and listening to the rain, savouring its smell, watching by torchlight the patterns the big, heavy raindrops made on the sand. Kai told her that the special, earthy scent of the rain was called petrichor. She hadn't known that. The rain stopped after ten minutes and she again lay back out under the stars and slid back into sleep.

She was awoken by Kai, kissing her on the shoulder and suggesting she wake up. 'Look,' he said, pointing out to sea.

Sienna didn't know where she was for a moment, but she quickly oriented herself and gasped in awe at the sight of a huge golden sun rising out of the sea. It tinted a scattering of low-hanging clouds to a blazing gold, and lit a pathway on the water that led straight to them and gilded Kai's smooth brown body with the rays that were bringing daylight to his island.

'Wow, just wow,' she breathed. 'If I'd known how awe-inspiring the sunrise was here, that would have been on the bucket list too.'

'You've now seen the sunset and the sunrise, these islands at their best.'

No, she thought but didn't dare say, the best sight of the islands was him.

The tide had come in and the water was much closer to them, the sea calmer with a low swell. She could taste salt in her mouth and nose, no doubt from breathing in the salt-laden air all night. Just for this moment she was an integral part of this landscape—she and Kai.

'I will never, ever forget this time here with you,' she said. He kissed her and kisses quickly led to lovemaking, urgent and energetic. Sex had become a revelation.

'Let's swim,' he said afterwards. 'There are few things more exhilarating than swimming naked in the surf with nothing between you and the water.'

Already Sienna knew that wasn't true. Nothing could be more exhilarating than making love with this man. Still, she ran hand in hand with him into the water and discovered the joy of swimming naked, as Kai had promised.

Neither of them spoke on the way back up to the house. Words would break the perfection of the moment, the finale to her bucket-list achievement. In reality, two bucket-list achievements— one spoken, to sleep under the stars, and the other unspoken: *have mind-blowing sex with a gorgeous, kind man*. For despite the stars and the sunrise and the raindrops, the real joy had been Kai. Not just the great sex—and it had been great to the point she had felt moved to a different plane of being—but his thoughtfulness towards her. That thoughtfulness and anticipation of her needs had led to the fulfilling sex. But this time with him could well be as ephemeral as those shooting stars upon which she'd wished so fervently. The thought was unbearable. She'd only known him for a few days; she shouldn't be feeling such a strong emotional attachment. She had to gird herself to the reality there could be no future to this. Once back in London, it would all seem like a dream.

Kai.

'Are you sure I look all right?' she said after she'd showered and dressed in her shorts and new pineapple T-shirt. Thankfully, she had brought basic makeup in her toiletries bag. The thought of meeting Kai's daughter and grandparents was nerve-racking in the extreme.

'You don't just look *all right*…you look beautiful,' he said, running his finger down her cheek. She took his hand and kissed it.

'I feel bad that I don't have something to take for your grandmother. My sisters and I were brought up never to go empty-handed as a guest to someone else's house.'

'My grandmother knows the circumstances of your visit.'

'That I've stayed the night on the island with you?'

'Why not? We're in our thirties, not teenagers. She'll consider what we do alone to be entirely our business.'

'I'm very pleased with what we did alone on the island.'

'Me too.' He pulled her to him in a hug; she closed her eyes at the bliss of it. She loved the feeling of his strong arms wrapped protectively around her; wished she could stay there forever.

He released her. 'C'mon, let's get going. I'm starving and the food is always good at my grandmother's house. It won't take long to get there in the boat.'

One thing she had learned about Kai, he was a man of large appetites and she had acquired a voracious appetite for him.

CHAPTER ELEVEN

APART FROM THE house and a few small outbuildings, Kai's *motu* was undeveloped, with no landscaping to speak of, and that was a major part of its charm, Sienna thought. Not so his grandparents' house on their private *motu*, which was something altogether more sophisticated.

Several luxury boats were moored at the commercial-size dock. To get to the house, she and Kai had to follow a path through palm trees that led to a bridge across a lagoon planted with water lilies and lotus, pink and white flowers rising above large, flat leaves. They disturbed a graceful white waterbird, and it took off with a splash to fly up past a tree over a canopy clustered with bright red tropical flowers. The air was redolent with the scent of a *tiare* hedge planted along the pathway, the Tahitian gardenia with its small white flowers and glossy green leaves.

They turned a corner and the house was upon

them, a very high thatched roof with timber walls nestled into the landscape. 'I'm seriously impressed by your grandparents' place,' she said.

'The house is built in the traditional Polynesian *faré* style—I thought you'd be interested.'

'Everything is incredible, the grounds, the lagoon, that awesome thatched roof.'

'It's what I grew up with,' he said.

She thought of the house where she grew up in Chiswick, on a suburban London street lined with similar Edwardian-style houses—the contrast could not be greater. How starkly it underlined the differences in their worlds.

'This is where you came to live when you left your parents' house?' she asked.

She wondered what their house looked like in Papeete; she suspected it was a large house in the best part of town. It wasn't that she judged people by their houses—she was an interior designer; houses and the way people lived in them interested her.

'I have separate quarters behind the main house,' Kai said. 'The traditional *faré* style has different living areas in separate smaller buildings.'

'I'd love to find out more about that style of architecture, how it evolved to suit the environment.'

'And an extended family,' he said.

The house was incredible inside, soaring thatch ceilings, walls of woven bamboo, amazing artworks and sculptures she'd like to look at more closely. As a designer, she had to stop herself from gawking. Kai might be a wealthy man in his own right, but he obviously came from a family of some standing.

Kai let them in and the first person she met as they headed towards the main living area was Kinny. Kai's daughter toddled towards her father to launch herself at his legs where she hugged him tight. 'Papa!'

Kai laughed as he swung her up into his arms and kissed her on each cheek. *'Ma poupette.'* Sienna knew that translated to 'my little doll' as an endearment.

This was definitely the adorable baby she had seen on the beach with a mop of curly brown hair, big brown eyes and a heart-shaped face. She stuck her thumb in her mouth and looked solemnly at Sienna. Sienna thought how natural Kai looked with his child in his arms. And how very much like Kai his daughter looked. No wonder he hadn't doubted her paternity.

'Bonjour, Kinny, je m'appelle Sienna.' She thought she should try and speak French to introduce herself.

'She's learning to speak English at the same time as French,' Kai said, looking proudly at his sweet daughter. 'We're trying to discourage her from sucking her thumb, though.'

'I sucked my thumb until I went to school, and it didn't harm my teeth,' Sienna said, then immediately wished she hadn't. 'Sorry, I didn't mean to contradict your parenting methods.'

'Everyone has their opinion,' he said. 'But it's good to know sucking your thumb didn't do you any harm.'

Then his grandmother, Heiani, was there, warm, vibrant, with a mass of curly silver hair tucked behind her ears with brilliant pink hibiscus flowers, wearing a casual dress brightly patterned in red and pink. She spoke English with a charming French accent. '*Maeva*...welcome,' she said. 'You must be hungry.'

'We were up with the sun and swimming, so yes, we are,' Kai said.

After introductions were made, Heiani switched her focus to Sienna. 'So you are the one,' Heiani said slowly.

'I'm sorry?' Sienna said, caught by the older woman's dark eyes. For a long moment she couldn't look away, mesmerised, like that first time with Kai.

'I meant the one who employed Kai as a kite-surfing instructor,' Heiani said, looking away, but for some reason, Sienna didn't think she'd meant that at all.

Sienna flushed. 'I'm sorry. I had no idea who he was when I asked him to teach me, and he didn't tell me until after the lesson.'

'My grandson is humble about his achievements. Humility and having a big heart are important qualities in Polynesian people. He has both in abundance.'

Sienna looked over to Kai and Kinny. 'I have learned that about him.' She had never imagined a man like Kai existed.

'I'm sure you also noticed he is the most handsome of my grandsons,' Heiani said with a fond look at Kai as he tucked Kinny on his hip.

'I most certainly did,' Sienna said, unable to stop a soft, besotted smile as she took in his warm eyes and spectacular smile, and thought about how good he'd been to her and what an amazing lover he had proved to be. When she'd first noticed him, it had been his looks that had attracted her, but now she knew him as a person, his good looks went soul deep.

She realised his grandmother had caught the smile and her blush deepened. Sienna concentrated on an interesting wooden carving hanging on the closest wall. What did Heiani really think of her grandson bringing a guest from her resort to her home?

Heiani told them that breakfast was ready and

Kai showed Sienna the way. 'Kinny is enchanting,' she told him.

'Aren't you?' she said to the little girl, who giggled.

'Do you think she understands me?'

'She understands many more words than she actually says,' Kai said, 'but she obviously feels comfortable with you.'

'I'm glad,' she said.

'Now she wants to get down and run after her great-grandmother,' he said as he placed her gently on the floor. Kinny toddled confidently after Heiani. 'Seems like she's on a mission.'

Breakfast was set out on a table on a shady balcony overlooking the lagoon and thence to the sea. They were joined by Kai's grandfather, Teri, a tall, broad-shouldered man with a warm smile and a quiet manner. Breakfast was served like a mini hotel buffet, with Tahitian and Western choices of meal and a maid serving coffee and other drinks. That was perhaps not surprising, Sienna thought, as Heiani and Teri owned a renowned resort and had a team of housekeepers at home. She didn't think she could cope with a traditional raw fish dish at that time of the morning; she would choose instead from fresh tropical fruit, yogurt, granola, banana pancakes, cold meats, baguettes and twisty Tahitian doughnuts known as *firi-firi*.

Before they sat down to eat, Kai spoke softly to her, 'I believe Kinny has something for you.'

The little girl walked carefully towards her with some red hibiscus flowers in her hand. She held up her arms to Sienna. 'Up,' she said imperiously.

Sienna looked to Kai. 'Is it all right if I pick her up?'

He nodded.

She lifted the tiny girl up and propped her on her hip as she had seen so many mothers do. Kinny was such a welcome warm weight in her arms and Sienna felt her heart thud with longing. She was thirty-two; she could have expected to have a child Kinny's age by now, possibly more than one. Kinny smiled, showing tiny first teeth. Safely in the circle of Sienna's arms, she indicated for Sienna to bend her head to her then she reached out and tucked a hibiscus behind each of Sienna's ears. 'For you,' she said.

'Thank you, Kinny,' Sienna said, more than a little bit choked up. 'How kind of you.'

Kai was watching her and his daughter with an indulgent smile. 'Good girl, Kinny,' he said. 'The flowers look beautiful on Sienna. She looks like a Polynesian lady now.'

'Is it okay if I kiss Kinny?' Sienna asked Kai.

'Of course,' he said.

She kissed the precious little girl lightly on

each cheek in the French way, *la bise*, as she had seen Kai do, and breathed in her sweet baby scent, like apples and honey. She wasn't prepared for the rush to her heart when Kinny put her little arms around her neck and kissed her back.

'Thank you, Kinny,' she said, her voice a little choked. Was it possible for her womb to actually ache with longing for a baby of her own? A baby just like this one?

Kinny kissed her again and then giggled— surely one of the most delightful sounds it was possible to hear. Then the little girl let it be known she wanted to get down. Sienna's arms felt empty without her and she had to close her eyes against a sudden sense of loss. She felt Heiani's gaze on her but she couldn't hide her feelings.

Kai put Kinny in a booster seat at the table between him and his grandmother where they could help her with her breakfast. The little girl was fiercely independent and had strong views of what foods she liked and didn't like. Like she herself had been as a child, Sienna thought, so her parents said.

'Kinny likes you,' Kai said. 'She's a friendly, open child but she can be shy with strangers. She's taken to you in a big way.'

'I hope so,' she said. 'Because I like her very much. What a precious gift she was to you.'

'Absolutely a treasure,' he said. 'I'm a fortunate man.'

'And Kinny has a wonderful papa,' she said to a nod of approval from Heiani.

After they'd finished eating, Teri excused himself as he wanted to head over to the resort. Sienna liked the way he kissed his wife goodbye as her parents always did. These were the loving people who had taken in their grandson and nurtured his dreams, the dreams his own parents had seen no value in. Not for the first time, she gave thanks for her parents and her sisters. She only had one grandparent, her nana, who was a potter of some renown living in Dorset. Her mother always said that was where Sienna's creative talents had come from. Nana used to come up to London for Christmas, and helped with Eliza when she was needed throughout the year. These days she didn't care for the journey and the family went to her after Christmas. Sienna was due for a visit.

Heiani turned to Sienna and Kai. 'We're looking forward to having you with us for Christmas Day.'

'Thank you so much for inviting me,' Sienna said. 'I was dreading spending Christmas Day on my own. Not that your resort won't put on a Christmas feast,' she hastily added.

'But it's not the same as being with family

and friends, and Kai tells me you usually spend Christmas with them.'

'Yes, we're a close family but I know I'll enjoy being with you. I've never spent Christmas in another country. Also, we don't have any children in our family, so it will be a bonus to be with Kinny and your other great-grandchildren.'

'Christmas is always magical when viewed through the eyes of children,' Heiani said. 'It's not the same without them.'

Each word was like a stab to the heart. 'No, it isn't,' she said, forcing her voice to sound even.

'Has Kai told you about the Christmas parade on Saturday? We will be taking Kinny to the parade. You must join us.'

'If Sienna wants to go, Mama'u,' Kai said.

'Sienna wants to,' Sienna said quickly, which made them all laugh.

She was enjoying it here with his family and his daughter. There was the same kind of warmth and acceptance as she found in her own family. She caught Kai's gaze, saw the understanding and the kindness there, remembered the passion and the fierceness too. Her heart seemed to turn over.

She was falling in love with him.

This was not—never had been—a holiday fling. This—Kai—was rather more than great sex and the fact she admired him as a father.

And now she was halfway to falling in love with his baby daughter. But where could it go to?

'Today I'm taking Sienna to Vaitape to visit Uncle Rai's jewellery store and do some Christmas shopping.'

'Perhaps you might like to help us decorate the Christmas tree on Saturday, Sienna?' Heiani asked. 'Then go with us to the Parade de Noel.'

'I…I would be honoured,' Sienna said, happy to be included, but at the same time a little panicked. The closer she got to Kai and Kinny, the harder it would be to say goodbye.

'The Parade de Noel is a Christmas pageant in Vaitape, which is fun. Lots of traditional singing and dancing and a parade. I think you'd like it,' Kai explained. 'Kinny will be enthralled by it.'

'It sounds fun. Something very different to the way I've always celebrated Christmas. For one thing, Christmas has always meant cold weather for me, all bundled up in winter clothes.'

'This year you'll be dancing on the streets in a *pareo*,' Kai said.

Sienna couldn't meet his eyes in front of his perceptive grandmother—not when she remembered how he'd thought her gift wrapped in her *pareo*, and the way he had unwrapped her. He had made her feel sensations she'd never felt before—not just in her body but in her heart.

While she welcomed the chance to spend time with him together with his family, would there be time for them to be alone in the precious few days she had left with him?

Kai held Kinny in his arms as he and Sienna stood shoulder to shoulder to say goodbye to his grandmother. Kinny tried to say, 'Bye-bye, Sienna,' and couldn't quite pronounce the unfamiliar name.

Sienna laughed and leaned over to kiss his little daughter. 'Bye-bye, Kinny, you darling girl.'

The three of them together looked like a family. He knew it. His grandmother knew it. He didn't know if the thought had crossed Sienna's mind.

He was pleased at the way she fitted in so well with his grandparents—his grandmother hadn't had to say a word for him to know she approved. Approved big time, if all those sideways glances meant anything, although she knew her grandson well enough not to push him. Then there were the invitations to join the family for other activities that really let him know she approved.

Kinny needs a mother. How many times had his grandmother said that?

Her opinion was important. But what was more important was how Sienna was with Kinny, and Kinny with her. And that had gone well beyond expectation.

His daughter was a friendly child but could be shy with strangers. Not so with Sienna. Kinny had straightaway identified Sienna as a friend. Kai wondered if her reaction might have been because Sienna reminded her of her late mother, even though she had been only six months old the last time she had seen Paige. Kinny's mother had had similar colouring to Sienna, only with hazel eyes, not Sienna's incredible clear green eyes.

Or maybe she'd reacted that way because children naturally gravitated to young people; Kinny adored her young French cousins. His daughter spent much of her time with her great-grandparents and other older people. Or did Kinny sense that same thing he had sensed in Sienna, that she could be important to her? Had Sienna felt something of the same? He noticed she found it difficult to keep her eyes off Kinny. What did she think about children? They'd had so little time together to talk about important things like what they wanted to do with the rest of their lives and whether that might include children. Or how she felt about being a mother to another woman's child. Things that might take them beyond a fun, sexy fling.

Kai had been shocked by the reaction of some

of the people he knew when they'd found out about Kinny. 'A baby? That will cramp your style,' had been a common reaction. Not to mention, 'You can always put her up for adoption.' Not for a moment had he considered giving Kinny away. Not for a moment would his grandparents have let him consider it. Bonds of family and kinship were too deep and strong for that ever to have been a possibility.

He had been grappling with finding a balance among Kinny's needs, the demands of Wave Hunters and a life for himself. Along had come the wild card—Sienna. And now to be with her had become all he could think of. He had to find a way for her to be part of his life—and not become a memory of an island fling.

But how could it possibly work?

CHAPTER TWELVE

SIENNA LIKED SHOPPING. In fact, she didn't believe she could be good at her job if she didn't like shopping. Discovering new products and innovations was important for her design commissions and essential for the social media side of her business. Sometimes that perfect lamp or cushion or mirror was what gave just the right individual touch to the design of a room and lifted it from good to gorgeous. Not to mention less glamorous essentials such as mouldings, architraves, door furniture and bathroom fittings that had to be just right. She designed interiors down to the tiniest detail. And fabric— she loved fabrics and textiles. She also loved the trims, braiding, ribbons, tassels and beading that were the icing on an interior's cake, the collective name for which was *passementerie*, a word she simply adored.

She not only haunted French flea markets, but was also familiar with the best places to shop for everything interiors in London. She trawled the exclusive showrooms at the Chelsea Harbour Design Centre, as well as trade fairs, galleries, antique dealers from Mayfair to Islington and everywhere in between, student exhibitions, artisan markets and the bargain basements of upscale department stores. Then there were the vast worldwide shopping resources of the internet to call upon in her search for just the right thing for just the right place.

She couldn't use that excuse for clothes shopping, which was also a favourite pastime, although there was the excuse of having to look the part of a successful interior designer on her social media. However, it was the excuse of buying a necklace for her mother that had brought her—after a trip back to her resort to change—into the treasure trove of Tahitian black pearls that was the jewellery store owned by Kai's Uncle Rai. She was surrounded by the most exquisite pearls in colours that sang to her of those aquamarine waters that had given her such joy on this visit to Bora Bora.

Uncle Rai was Kai's grandparents' age, with short grey hair, a neatly trimmed beard and a charming manner. 'What do you know about Tahitian black pearls?' he asked her.

'Nothing. Except that they're very beautiful,' she said. 'Oh, and that they're produced inside an oyster shell.'

Kai laughed. 'Be prepared to learn everything you need to know and then some about Tahitian pearls. Uncle Rai is an expert.'

'Straightaway I have a question, Rai. They're called 'black' pearls, yet before I even start looking around properly, I can see they're not all black. Why is that?' Sienna asked.

'You're quite right,' Rai said. 'The Tahitian pearl is called 'black' but the colours range from jet-black through iridescent shades that include blue, purple, pink, silver, brown, green, cream, bronze and yellow. There are undertones and overtones that give further variation.'

'Are they artificially tinted inside the shell to get that range of colours?' Sienna realised she sounded like she was interviewing Rai, which gave her an idea.

Rai looked shocked. 'No. Never. All the colours are entirely natural and produced by the oyster itself—the giant, black-lipped mollusc that is indigenous only to the waters of French Polynesia. That natural process accounts for the varying shapes of the pearls too. Only rarely are they perfectly spherical.' Uncle Rai sounded like he was replying to her interview question—he was a natural.

'But the black pearls are the most valuable?' she said. She was super-aware of Kai, standing by and looking amused at her interrogation of his uncle.

'The rarest and most valuable colour is dark

green with peacock overtones like the shimmering of an oil slick. Green pearls are extremely beautiful. I will show you when I take you to our VIP room.'

An entire corner of the front showroom was devoted to a display of how the precious 'gems of the sea' were grown on underwater farms off various French Polynesian islands. The display included a screen with a video on a loop showing one of the smaller pearl farms in operation. The process started with the 'seeding' of the mature oyster with a piece of shell nucleus that it would coat with layers of the 'nacre' that formed the pearl. Through the growing period of two years, the oysters lived a protected life on long net panels in the sea until the pearls were harvested. It was all very labour-intensive and highly skilled. Sienna found it fascinating.

There were also actual samples of the giant, black-lipped oyster in which the cultured pearls were grown. Sienna was amazed to see some of the shells were nearly the size of a dinner plate. No wonder the Tahitian pearls were renowned for being bigger than from other pearl-producing places around the world.

'This might sound a silly question, but do the pearl farmers have favourite oysters that give them particularly good pearls?' she said.

'Not silly. It takes about two years for the mollusc to grow a pearl so theoretically an oyster can produce over a few cycles. But important to the quality of the pearl is its shine. As the mother of pearl—that's what we call a pearl-producing mollusc—gets older the pearls she produces get duller and hence less valuable.' Sienna decided she wouldn't tell her mother that story.

Sienna turned to Uncle Rai. She had to stop thinking of him as uncle, or she'd find herself calling him that instead of Rai. Yet she couldn't help feeling a connection with Kai's family; they were so welcoming.

'I'm finding this all so interesting. And I'm sure I'll find looking at the actual jewellery even more so. The thing is I'm an interior designer with a substantial following on social media, and I think my followers would find Tahitian black pearls interesting too. The pearls are so visually entrancing. Could I do a quick interview with you and post it online?'

'When she says *substantial*, she means over a million followers,' Kai said.

'Of course,' Rai said. 'I would be pleased to.'

Kai had told her some of the celebrities and very wealthy people who vacationed in Bora Bora often took pearls home with them from his uncle's store. But exposure to over a million people looking for design direction on social media wouldn't hurt his business.

'I thought you were meant to be on holiday and not working,' Kai said.

'Almost impossible for me not to, I'm afraid,' she said in mock apology. 'I only lasted a few days without getting my phone out. I've shot quite a few images to post when I get home. I even sourced those bamboo chairs I admired at the beach bar. It's difficult to switch off completely when you love your job so much it doesn't seem like a job.' Sadly, she'd never had a chance to photograph his beach house on Motu Puaiti. They'd found way more thrilling ways to pass the time.

'I won't tell your sisters you broke the work ban if you don't,' he joked.

Of course he didn't know her sisters; most likely he never would. Kai was a secret she wanted to hug to herself. She hadn't mentioned him to her sisters in any of her messages. Just a quick text this morning that the kitesurfing instructor had also taught her to surf. Nothing about his private island, or making love with him under the stars. Certainly not that she had fallen in love with him but was fighting it because she could not see it lasting outside of the magical environs of this Pacific paradise.

'I'd appreciate that,' she said. 'But everywhere I look here there's a photo of something I'm sure my followers would appreciate. I'm on holiday and I won't try to hide that. My posts are quite personal. My very first video post had me with my hair covered in white plaster dust when a wall nearly collapsed on me. It went viral.'

'I'm sure that made you more accessible.' He turned to his uncle. 'She might make you a star, Uncle Rai.'

'The pearls will be the star,' said his uncle very seriously.

She wished she hadn't brought up her business—work meant going home, and going home meant leaving Kai behind. Unless… Unless they tried to see each other again afterwards. But she had never known a long-distance relationship to work, no matter how many resolves were made. Best to enjoy every moment she could before she had to say goodbye and go back to 'real' life. Heartbreaking as the prospect was. She was such a late starter novice at dating, she didn't know how to deal with a relationship that had a limited life span.

Her social media videos never went more than a minute. It didn't take long to get a few sound bites from Rai and to shoot a few images of the production display. Then they headed to the VIP room at the back of the showroom.

'Why the VIP room?' she asked.

'It's more informal, private, secure and you can try pieces on in more comfort and privacy,' said Rai.

After an hour of happy browsing, Sienna settled on a single strand of purplish-toned semi-round pearls for her mother.

'An excellent choice,' Rai said.

'She's quite conservative and wears a lot of navy. I think she will love this. I'm very pleased.' Rai had substantially discounted the price too.

She bought pearl earrings for Thea and Eliza. An interesting pendant with a single, irregular-shaped baroque black pearl set in a tiny, stylised silver oyster shell for herself. And, hold that order, some earrings for herself too. She couldn't resist.

'You can be assured you're getting the best quality at the best price,' Rai said.

'Thank you. I appreciate that.' Kai's family helping her buy presents for her family. Who would have thought?

'I really like the more contemporary styles to shoot for my socials,' she said. 'Who designs them?'

'My granddaughter,' he said. 'She went to design school in Paris.'

'Even more interesting for my shoot,' she said. 'I'm getting quite excited about posting it.'

'What about those green pearls, the most prized ones?' said Kai. 'I think Sienna would be interested in seeing them.'

The triple choker of large, perfectly matched luminous pearls in tones of green was breathtaking—so was the price tag, a staggering number of French Pacific francs, no less scary translated into British pounds.

'Try it on,' suggested Kai. 'It will go well with your green eyes.'

'I hardly dare,' she said as she stood in front of the full-length mirror.

'Let me.'

Kai carefully lifted her hair and fastened the choker at the back of her neck. His fingers brushed against her skin, sending shivers of awareness through her. She'd had no idea physical attraction could be this powerful. If Uncle Rai wasn't there, if they were somewhere private, she would twist in Kai's arms to face him, draw him to her to claim a kiss. And then... She shuddered with desire.

'Are my hands cold?' said Kai. He knew. The tone of his voice told him he knew exactly what even his slightest touch was arousing in her.

'Er...no,' she managed to choke out, hoping Uncle Rai was unaware of what was going on. Kai had introduced her as a friend.

She stood in front of the mirror to admire the necklace. It truly was the most exquisite piece of jewellery. While beautiful in its velvet-lined box, the choker came to life on her. The pearls seemed to be reflected in her eyes and contrasted with her creamy skin. She felt them warm on her as if they were somehow transferring an energy. She couldn't stop looking at her image in the mirror.

'It's as if the necklace was made for you,' said Kai.

He stood behind her, his image reflected in the mirror, his hands resting on her shoulders. His eyes narrowed. Was he feeling the same sharp awareness as she was? Rai had turned his back on them, putting something away in a cabinet. Kai leaned down to whisper huskily in her ear. 'I can imagine you wearing just the necklace and nothing else.'

She met his glance in the mirror, whispered back, 'Nothing else but a pair of high-heeled stilettos.'

Kai took a deep intake of breath, turned it into a cough and took a step back from her. Rai was watching them again. She suspected he was now in no doubt that she and his nephew were more than friends. She didn't care.

'Would you mind if I took a selfie of me in the necklace for my page?' she asked Rai. 'I think my followers would get a kick out of seeing me in this dream necklace.'

'Go ahead,' he said. 'I would like a copy to keep. As Kai said, it looks like the choker was custom made for you, the colour, the size, everything is perfect.'

She snapped a few selfies, perfectly angled. 'I'm fascinated watching you do that, with just that hint of a pout,' said Kai. 'You look almost like a different person.'

'Years of practice,' she said, aware her hand was trembling a little.

When she took the photo it had been as if she had seen herself reflected in the mirror naked, except for the necklace and a pair of glittering stilettos; Kai stood behind, magnificently nude, leaning over her, his brown skin, those bold tribal tattoos, black hair falling to his shoulders. Now *that* was a post that would go viral. But when she looked back up, they were both—of course—fully clothed, she in a cream off-the-shoulder top and a short linen skirt and he in a white open-necked shirt and canvas shorts.

She took a deep breath to steady herself before she took a still life of the necklace that might be useful for a future colour story, teamed perhaps with fabrics and ceramics.

It was lunchtime by the time she had taken some final shots of a series of small bowls Rai had filled with different-coloured loose pearls, like something from Aladdin's cave.

'What a striking photo,' Kai said. 'Clever you.'

She thanked Uncle Rai for all his help and accidentally called him Uncle Rai when she said goodbye. He laughed. 'It feels like you're already part of the family.'

Already?

CHAPTER THIRTEEN

AS SOON AS they got outside and clear of Uncle Rai's shop, Sienna pushed Kai up against a fence and kissed him hard. He kissed her back, just as hard, and held her tight.

She broke away, panting. 'I really needed to do that. What happened in there?'

'You wanted me, I wanted you. Simple.'

'It seemed more like…like a compulsion.'

Kai cradled her face in his hands and she looked up into his handsome, handsome face. 'That's what really wanting someone is like. Maybe you just haven't felt it before.'

'Or maybe it's you.'

'Maybe it's you. I haven't felt that strongly before either.'

'So it's *us*.'

'Yes, it's *us*. That's a good way to put it. We're well matched.'

Sienna realised only now how very badly matched she'd been with her ex-husband.

'I guess that as we are in the main street of

Vaitape, there's nothing we can do right now about that compulsion,' she said.

'There's always tonight,' he said. 'That is, if you would like to see me.'

'I want to see you.' She felt overwhelmed by a sudden panic that he might not want to see her.

'Good. I need to go home to be with Kinny, as I was away last night, but she eats early. I'll put her to bed and then I can bring the boat back. That we are seeing each other is no secret at Mareva. Let me know if there is somewhere you would like to go to have dinner.'

'Could we...well...?'

'What?'

'My time here is so short, I...I want to spend as much time with you as I can. Rather than going out to a restaurant, could we get room service in my villa?'

'A very good idea,' he said.

She realised she'd been holding her breath for his reply and she let it out in a *whoosh*. 'I'm glad you think so. In the meantime, we need to get lunch. I'd like to try eating at a *roulotte*. Do you recommend that?'

'One of our famous food trucks? For a quick lunch they can be very good. I'll take you to my favourite.'

The *roulotte* was an open-sided truck that had been converted to a kitchen, with a woven thatch roof over it, picturesque in its own way. It was surrounded by banana trees. There were mismatched café-style tables and chairs under the shade of the trees and a view over the water.

'The food smells fantastic,' she said as they seated themselves at a table. The table was rather rickety and propped up by a wad of cardboard under one leg, which somehow added to the fun of it.

'The menu is up on that chalkboard. Everything I've had here is good. There are some Chinese dishes here, too. Chinese is the third influence on our Tahitian cuisine.'

'What do you recommend?'

'I'm going to have the fish.'

'Cooked or raw?' She couldn't help the trepidation in her voice.

He laughed. 'I guess *poisson cru* does take getting used to.'

'And… And I liked it. But I don't eat a lot of raw fish in London.'

'I'm going to have the pan-fried fish fillet with *frites*.'

'So fish and chips? I'll have the *chow mein*.' She reached for her purse. 'Let me get this.'

'I insist you don't. You are my guest.'

'But—'

'No buts.' His tone commanded no arguing. She watched him as Kai lined up at the truck to order and pay for their lunch. Her heart turned over at how handsome he was—and somehow, now, familiar. They were lovers, but they were friends, too, and she felt totally at ease with him. He obviously knew the family that ran the food truck and they chatted away in French. This was his hometown, his grandparents probably knew everyone and he was a local hero surfing champion. His ties to the island were strong. As hers were to London.

He brought the food back to the table with bottles of sparkling mineral water.

'Thank you for taking me to Uncle Rai's,' she said. 'I hope you didn't mind me going into work mode like I did. I couldn't help it.'

'I enjoyed seeing you in action,' he said. 'I'll have to follow you on your socials so I can see how your pearl-shopping expedition looks when you post it.'

'Good idea,' she said. 'And if you make a nice comment on my posts that would be good. The more engagement with followers, the better.'

'Even with your large numbers?'

'It takes work to stay in front of my followers and to get new ones,' she said.

'I have a marketing department to handle all that for Wave Hunters, but I think they could learn from you.'

'We're all learning all the time, and hoping

the social media powers-that-be don't switch the rules on us.'

They finished lunch with fat, juicy mangoes bought from a basket on the food truck counter. 'I thoroughly enjoyed that, thank you,' she said. 'Before we head off to do some Christmas shopping, what shall I do about presents for your family on Christmas Day?'

'You're not expected to bring anything. The family exchanges gifts on Christmas Eve.'

'Still, I'd like to take something with me. A gift for your grandmother at the least. But what can I get from here that she wouldn't already have? If I was in London, it would be different.'

'Please don't be concerned. You're not expected to buy gifts for my family.'

'Maybe something for Kinny?'

'Perhaps something for Kinny.'

She wanted to get a Christmas present for him, too, but was faced with the same dilemma.

'Where to next?' he asked once they'd got up from the *roulotte* and were walking towards the shops.

'I'd like to get some Christmas decorations. Each year my parents and sisters all contribute a new ornament for the family Christmas tree. The tree was getting very full but a couple of years ago I was fostering a kitten who launched herself at the tree and brought it crashing down.

We still haven't caught up replacing all the ones that smashed. I'd like to get some from here. I saw a really cute little blown glass turtle ornament at one of the shops here the other day but there were too many people in there because a cruise ship had come in and I got fed up with waiting.'

'You foster cats?'

'Yes, however, that particular kitten was a foster fail. I ended up keeping her.'

'Where is she now?'

'Staying with a neighbour who boards cats. I'm lucky to have someone so close. Do you like cats or dogs?'

'I've never had the chance to have either, though I've wanted to. My parents weren't pet lovers. And my lifestyle doesn't lend itself to a pet. I guess I'd prefer a dog to a cat but as I've never had a cat I can't say.'

'I like dogs, too, but they don't fit with my life, either. But I really love my cat.' She paused. 'Please don't tell me she's a child substitute.'

'I wasn't going to say any such thing. But it leads to a question. You didn't have children with your ex-husband?'

She stopped. 'No.'

'I'm sorry. I shouldn't have asked.'

She looked straight ahead, not wanting to meet his gaze. 'It's okay. It's a reasonable question. I always wanted children. I…I wouldn't have married my ex if I'd believed he thought any differently. Seemed he changed his mind. It's one of the reasons the marriage ended. Apart from his multiple infidelities, that is.'

Kai cursed under his breath, the first time she had heard him do so. It sounded really powerful in French. He stopped, steered her towards the shade of a banana tree. She let herself be steered. This really wasn't the conversation to have walking along a public thoroughfare. 'Sienna, I—'

She put up her hand. 'Please. I shouldn't have said anything. I don't want to talk about it. I've put him behind me. But the children thing…that still hurts. You're so lucky to have Kinny. She is absolutely adorable. I'm quite smitten with her.'

And I'm totally smitten with you.

He pulled her into his arms and she went unresistingly. He was so strong and comforting. She closed her eyes to take in the sheer pleasure of being with him. Could there be a safer place in the world to be than in his arms?

'Kinny is smitten with you, too,' he said.

'If…if I'd had a child, I would have liked one just like her.'

'That's quite the compliment,' he said.

'She's quite the wonderful little person.'

This situation was hopeless. She was in love

with him, in love with his daughter, halfway in love with his heavenly country. But her life was in London. Just a taste of doing some work for her socials today had brought that home. So had buying gifts for her mother and sisters and imagining how they would react to them. Her life was nearly ten thousand miles away on the other side of the world.

She broke away from Kai's embrace and started to walk towards the shops again. She could enjoy Kai's company, Kinny's, too, and his family's for Christmas Day. But she couldn't let herself get too attached. She had to guard her heart. Bora Bora was a paradise and this—Kai, his little girl, his amazing house on his private island—was like a beautiful dream. She would have to wake up to reality.

She also had to face the thought that Kai might be looking for a mother for Kinny—having a wife to care for his child while he flitted around the world for Wave Hunters would solve a lot of his problems. She wasn't sure he was thinking that way—after all, he could well afford nannies to help him, not to mention that extended family—but it could never work for her. She loved what she did, and while being self-employed would make it easier to both keep up her career and be a mum, she had to be in England.

But she was running ahead of herself. Kai had made no mention of seeing her again after she went back home. In England, it might be significant for a man to take a woman home to meet his child and family. Here, she realised, they were way more friendly and hospitable, with the extended family a real thing. The houses were even designed to accommodate extra family members—like a baby dropped off at a hotel lobby welcomed in. His invitation might mean nothing more than making her welcome in a foreign country—Kai bringing his new friend along, as she was a tourist away from home on Christmas Day. Meeting his family might be of no significance whatsoever.

How simple it had been on Motu Puaiti. Just him and her with complete privacy and no obligations. Not to mention no clothes. But Kinny, his responsibilities—he was the billionaire head of his own global company for heaven's sake—Kai had to think of that. His grandparents had given him everything. He couldn't leave this place.

'Hah, I think this is the shop with the turtle Christmas ornament,' she said. 'It will be a big hit on the tree at home. For next year, that is.'

'Next year will you go back to the same family Christmas you've always had?'

'You know, I haven't even thought about that.

I just assumed we would. But just because I want it to be that way doesn't mean it will happen. Maybe… Maybe my parents were trying to tell us something by choosing to go away at Christmas.'

'And your sisters?'

'Who knows? Thea mentioned bumping into an old friend of hers on the Japanese ski slopes. He's someone I always thought she'd be great with as more than friends. She and Eliza are lovely, smart women. They're likely to end up with partners one day. Then Christmas might be very different.'

'And you? Do you see yourself with a husband one day?'

'No.' She was looking straight ahead and was glad he couldn't see her face. 'My marriage was hell at the end. I don't think I could ever trust a man again. I caught my ex in our bed with another woman and discovered he'd been cheating on me and gaslighting me for years. Thank heaven my father had made sure I'd kept my business dealings separate and my name on the title deeds of the house or he would have undermined me financially too.'

Again, a string of French expletives from Kai. She appreciated his vehemence.

'Not to mention I don't want to risk having to again give up my life, my interests, in favour of a husband's. That seems to be quite common in marriages.'

'Not all marriages.'

'But it's a risk, isn't it? My bucket-list wishes were ones I couldn't achieve while I was married. And how innocuous they were. Imagine letting someone mock your desire to sleep under the stars. In part, that was my fault—I let him get away with dominating me. It won't happen again. What about you?'

He paused. 'I have more than enough on my plate with Kinny and Wave Hunters to be considering any more commitments,' he stated flatly.

Oh. That was a clear statement of his position. She'd been misreading him. She was just an island fling after all—not just a fling, she knew it was more than that—but she was indeed reading too much into the visit to the grandparents' house this morning. It was contrary of her to feel a little hurt by it.

Who knew that beneath the athletic, sporty exterior of Sienna Kendall beat the heart of a relentless shopaholic? Kai couldn't help but be amused as he watched her shop for Christmas ornaments in the Vaitape village shops. She was like a hunter zeroing in on its prey. And all done in fluent French.

'I'm not just shopping for me,' she explained.

'As I've been invited to help trim your family's tree, I thought I might gift them with a few new ornaments too. I love the glass turtle so much. Surely your grandmother will too.'

'Kinny will like it, that's for sure.'

'I also like the palm tree and the pineapple. They're brilliant.'

As the glassblower who had made the ornaments happened to be in the store, of course she was videoed and interviewed for Sienna's socials as well. He was seeing a new side to Sienna today—the consummate businesswoman. She was both creative and canny. And, as she'd said, she loved her job so much it could hardly be regarded as work.

But his pleasure in her enthusiasm was bittersweet. She might like the snorkelling and the turtles and the kitesurfing here; she might like *him*, but her interests lay in a big city like London with proximity to Europe. Then there was the damage from her marriage—the wounds were deep; had they left permanent scars? Would she actually ever want to commit herself again? He and Kinny couldn't have less than total commitment.

As the meeting with Kinny had gone so well, he'd been letting his thoughts stray to the possibilities of a future with Sienna, but now it was seeming less and less likely. He had to put those thoughts aside and focus on enjoying the time he had left with her. Some things were simply not meant to be and he had to accept that.

'Kai, come and have a look at these toys. I've seen one I think Kinny might like.'

She dragged him off to another area of the shop. He went willingly, trying not to react with any emotion to the sight of this beautiful woman so excited at the idea of buying gifts for his little daughter, his daughter who had had such a sad start to life and had been so taken with Sienna.

She took him to a display of beautifully crafted wooden toys. 'They're made by a collective of carvers and craftspeople, from local sustainable timbers with nontoxic paints and glues. What do you think of this little train? Isn't it cute? There's a different carved animal sitting in each of the five open carriages. I love the little black-and-white cat because it reminds me of my own. The lady says it's perfect for Kinny's age and perfectly safe too. No small pieces to choke on and if she puts the pieces in her mouth they're safe.'

'I think she would love it.'

'Really? Then I'll buy it for her.'

'That's very thoughtful of you.'

She turned to the salesperson and completed the transaction in French.

'No interviewing the people who make them?' Kai said.

'Sadly, no. Seems they're on another island. But I'll get some good shots of the toys.'

'Anything else on the shopping list?' he said.

She looked at him through narrowed eyes. 'You've had enough of shopping, haven't you?'

'If there's more you want to see—'

'No. You've had enough. I can tell.'

He shrugged. 'I won't lie. You're right. I can leave you here if you want to shop more. You could get a taxi back to the resort or—'

'No,' she said vehemently. 'I don't want to waste one possible minute I could be spending with you. Just let me take a few shots of the toys. What would you like to do next?'

'Kitesurf. There's enough time.'

Her green eyes lit up. 'I would love that. I want to kitesurf as much as I can while I can. There'll never be an instructor as good as you.'

Was that what he was to her—a kitesurfing instructor and a convenient lover to introduce her to the good sex she seemed to have missed during the years of her bad marriage?

He couldn't—*wouldn't*—believe that was true.

CHAPTER FOURTEEN

THE CHRISTMAS TREE in Kai's grandparents' enormous living room was like nothing Sienna had ever seen before. It didn't resemble a traditional fir tree in any way. Rather, it was a tall abstract structure made of bamboo, sheets of woven pandanus, twisted palm leaves, tree branches and bunches of large, dried leaves. And she loved it.

'When I was shopping for Christmas ornaments, why didn't you warn me they wouldn't be for the traditional type of tree?' she asked Kai. 'The trees in the shops were just like the ones back home.'

'I thought you might like to be surprised by a Polynesian Christmas tree.'

'You certainly did that. As a designer, I like it a lot. It seems organic to the house, as if it belongs in the room. I somehow assumed—I don't know why as I'm in a different country with a different culture—that the tree would be a traditional fir one decorated with a collection of ornaments collected by the family over the years, like my family's tree. I don't think my glass turtle ornament—beautiful as it is—is going to be at all appropriate.'

'Think again,' Kai said with a smile. 'The tree isn't decorated yet. This is just the basic, untrimmed tree. My grandmother invited you to help trim the tree, didn't she?'

'She did. Before we go out to the Parade de Noel.'

'This is the support structure. Today we will put on the ornaments and baubles. Tomorrow it will be decorated with fresh foliage and fresh flowers. Frangipani blossoms will cover the tree. They will be replaced as they wilt.'

'What a wonderful idea. But how will we get those flowers on the tree?'

'That's not our job. The gardeners will do the flowers tomorrow, Christmas Eve. Now the family ornaments will go on as usual, as they did in the days we had a traditional tree. Including some appalling decorations I made in primary school.'

'Really? We have ones I made at school on our tree at home too. It's very embarrassing.'

Kai laughed. 'My grandmother refuses to throw them out.'

Then Heiani, Kai's grandmother, was there, with Kinny in her arms. 'So nice you are here, Sienna,' she said.

'Sienna…' Kinny said in her sweet baby voice.

Sienna looked at Kai, who shrugged. 'I didn't teach her that.'

'I did,' said Heiani. 'She should know how to pronounce the name of an honoured guest.'

'Thank you,' Sienna said, touched. 'And thank you, too, Kinny.'

'Sienna,' Kinny said again and put out her arms to Sienna from where she was held in her grandmother's arms.

Sienna looked from Kai to Heiani.

'She wants to go to you,' said Kai, sounding pleased.

'I will gladly take her,' Sienna said.

Heiani handed over her great-granddaughter, and Sienna's arms were full of cuddly little girl. Her heart flipped over. 'Hi, Kinny, precious little one,' she said. Kinny kissed her on the cheeks, then put out her arms to her father. 'Your turn, Papa,' Sienna said, handing her over to Kai.

'I think I'm offended that I seem to be her number two,' Kai said, looking fondly at his daughter as he took her into his arms.

Sienna went to her tote bag. 'I brought some ornaments for the tree with me. As a gift, I mean, if that's okay. I bought them in Vaitape,' she said to Heiani. 'They're hand-blown glass. I met the artist.' She spoke too quickly. Even though Heiani had been nothing but welcoming, she felt a little nervous around her.

'You didn't need to do that, but thank you,' Heiani said.

'Here they are. Maybe you could decide which one to give Kinny to put on the tree.' She handed them to her, each in a soft, padded pouch.

Heiani took them out of the pouches, one by one and laid them on the table. 'They're beautiful. Works of art.'

'I thought so too. I have the same four to take home with me.'

'I think Kinny might like the turtle best, although she will have to be strictly supervised hanging it on the tree—it is, after all, glass. The others are lovely too. It's hard to choose which one I like best between the pineapple, the palm tree and the dolphin.' Each had a silk cord to hang it from the tree.

'They're all for you, for your tree, if you want them, of course.'

Heiani smiled. 'Thank you. That was very thoughtful of you. Always nice to have some new ornaments. We'll think of you every time they go on the tree.'

Or would she be long forgotten by next Christmas?

'I'm glad you like them. The turtle is my favourite too. It will always make me think of the turtles that swim in these waters.'

A maid brought in a tray with cold drinks and snacks. Then Kai's grandfather, Teri, joined them. 'Would Kinny like to put the first ornament on the tree?' he said. He was as besotted with the little girl as everyone else. Her mother, Paige, had done the absolute best thing in bringing her baby to her father's family.

Sienna stood near as Kai held Kinny up to the tree and helped her hang the silk loop over a branch. It wasn't as successful as everyone thought. Kinny liked the turtle and wanted to keep it, not leave it on the tree. An impressive tantrum ensued. Who knew a baby of eighteen months old could make such a noise?

Sienna asked if she could distract Kinny with the gift of the wooden train set. It was an immediate hit, which pleased Sienna—and gained her kudos from the grandparents. Kinny fell asleep playing with it on the floor nearby them, a cushion tucked under her head.

Then the adults put up the collection of ornaments, going back many years, deciding which was the best place for each. Many were the classic glass baubles that made up a lot of the Kendall family collection, too—although there had been more of them before the kitten attack.

'I'm looking forward to seeing the rest of the

tree covered in flowers,' Sienna said. 'What a beautiful tradition.'

'We had a designer working at the resort one year and she suggested we try a different kind of contemporary tree, more environmentally appropriate to our part of the world, like this one. It was a hit with the guests. From then on, we've had one at home too.'

Sienna hadn't taken much notice of the Christmas decorations at the resort. She'd been too busy making the most of every moment with Kai. Yesterday they'd had the entire day and night to themselves. When they hadn't been kitesurfing, they'd taken bikes out to explore the inland. The rest of the time they'd stayed in her villa, ordered room service and didn't get out of bed. She'd been surprised how nice it was to do something as everyday as watch a movie and eat pizza with him.

Although she tried to barricade her heart, she fell more and more in love with Kai every minute she spent with him but, as if by unspoken agreement, they avoided any talk of the future. She still wasn't sure if he felt in any way the same towards her, but he treated her with such respect she didn't question it.

After all the decorations had found homes on the tree—she was pleased how good the ones she had bought looked—they shared a light meal so, Heiani said, they wouldn't have to battle the crowds in Vaitape. The maid served up chicken and fish that had been wrapped in leaves and herbs and steamed in an underground oven called an *ahima'a* in the Polynesian way. They finished with *po'e*, a sweet, cold dessert made with banana and brown sugar and served with coconut cream. Sienna thought it a privilege to share traditionally cooked food in a private home, an experience not many tourists would enjoy.

After dinner Heiani told them she was tired and she and Teri were going to miss the Christmas parade. Why didn't Kai and Sienna take Kinny out to the parade on their own?

Sienna glanced to Kai and he nodded. 'The festivities start at sunset, so we should be going now.'

'I'm ready,' she said.

'Kinny's bag is already packed,' Heiani said.

'You know I haven't a clue how to look after her,' Sienna said, feeling vaguely panicky. 'I have no idea how to change a nappy or give a bottle.'

'Kinny's way past bottles,' said Heiani. 'You don't need to worry. Kai knows how to look after his daughter. Just have fun.'

Her brown eyes twinkled and for a moment Sienna wondered if Heiani was actually tired at all, or was sending Kai and Sienna out with Kinny on their own—like a little family.

As the speedboat approached Vaitape, with Kai at the wheel and Kinny safely strapped in both harness and lifejacket, Sienna could hear the sounds of the parade floating across the water: singing, drums, the Tahitian ukulele, guitars. Kinny started chortling and waving her hands around in delight.

'This sounds like it will be fun, Kai,' Sienna said.

'It's a real community thing,' he said. 'People come in from small, remote islands and atolls to let their hair down and enjoy themselves. All to the backdrop of the last of the sunset.'

It was an exceptional sunset, the sun tinting the clouds multiple colours in contrast to the few dark storm clouds persisting in the sky. Sienna hoped it wouldn't rain on these people's parade but if it did, she suspected they would simply dance on.

Kai killed the engine and docked the boat. 'Are you ready to watch the parade and dance in the street?'

'My feet are itching to,' she said.

The parade made its way down the main street of Vaitape, the streets lined with well-wishers. The floats represented various aspects of town and country life both past and present. Sienna didn't know what they represented but she cheered them anyway.

People were dancing in traditional clothes, grass skirts, extravagant headdresses made from palm leaves and brightly coloured flowers, floral leis, the women beautiful, the men muscular and graceful. The scent of frangipani and *tiare* mixed with the cooking smells coming from the *roulottes* and the fuel from the flares that lit the darkness. Immense cheers went up for the float for Mr Bora Bora and Miss Bora Bora, two impossibly beautiful young people laughing their happiness and excitement.

Kinny was secured in a hiking carrier on Kai's back, at a good height for her to be able to look around. He caught Sienna's hand and danced with her, with Kinny on his back, the three of them together. Like a family. The people were friendly. Normally, she didn't care for crowds but here she felt safe and part of it all. They treated them like a little family, making sure Kinny had a good view of the parade. For a moment Sienna let herself give in to the fantasy. How did it feel to be a family? This family? Could it ever be?

Kai groaned inwardly. He was getting more and more attached to Sienna, but still could not see where their relationship—it really, truly wasn't a fling—could go. He'd enjoyed tonight at the parade more than he could ever remember enjoying it, seeing it through the eyes of Sienna and his baby daughter. Kinny was obviously very happy to be with Sienna. She kept repeating her newly learned name, so pleased with herself, laughing every time she said it. 'Sienna.'

Finally, they took Kinny home. He and Sienna put her to bed. Sienna sat by the side of the bed and gently stroked his daughter's cheek until she fell asleep. 'How can you bear to leave her when you go away?' she said.

'It's getting more and more difficult,' he said. 'I feel I miss so much of her development when I'm only a few weeks away from her.'

He invited Sienna to stay over in his quarters but she asked him to take her back to her villa. Tomorrow was a family day for him and she would bow out. He should have dropped her and turned straight back home. But he couldn't bear to leave her. He walked her to her villa and stayed. There was an urgency to their lovemaking, knowing their time was limited.

He left her sleeping, her hair spread out on the pillow, one arm flung above her head. She was beautiful. He loved her.

He couldn't let her go.

He had to think of some way to keep her in his life.

* * *

On Christmas Eve Sienna woke alone. She had been invited for Christmas Eve dinner with Kai's family, but she had declined. She knew they exchanged gifts in the evening and she felt it was a family time. She had no status in the family—not girlfriend, not colleague, not even a friend—and felt she shouldn't be there, although she appreciated their kindness in inviting her.

She knew there were tensions, too, between Kai and his parents, and she didn't want to be an awkward onlooker to that. Truth be told, she was dreading meeting his parents. Heiani and Teri were inclusive, welcoming people— Kai's parents sounded rigid and conservative; the father wouldn't even acknowledge adorable Kinny.

Christmas Day would be different. She wouldn't feel out of place there. Her family had a tradition of inviting people who were alone on Christmas Day, and this year she would be one of them— with another family on the other side of the world.

Also, she had to pack and get ready to leave Bora Bora as she was leaving early Boxing Day morning. The suitcase her sisters had packed for her was a little heavier with the gifts she had bought them—and herself. The resort boat would take her to the small island airport for the flight to Papeete, then Los Angeles and finally

London. She dreaded having to say goodbye not just to Kai but to Kinny too.

But there was still Christmas Day to come.

The shops were still open on Christmas Eve and the town was full of the sound of pealing church bells and choir song. She didn't know what she could get as a gift for Kai. He was a billionaire with all those resources available to him. Everything in the shops here was basically for tourists; there was nothing she thought he would need or want. But she could not leave Bora Bora without getting him a present. She wanted him to remember her, even if only fleetingly.

She went back to Uncle Rai's jewellery shop. Uncle Rai wasn't there but a very pleasant young man served her. She knew what she wanted, she'd seen it there the other day, had nearly asked Kai if he liked it. It was a men's wrist strap made with twists of black leather, a single very black pearl and a heavy antique silver clasp. It was a very handsome piece. She was on the database as a client and was surprised and pleased to get a discount. Kai's family looked after their own. But she wasn't part of the family; Kai wasn't hers. Yet the thought of leaving him spiralled her into despair.

CHAPTER FIFTEEN

ON CHRISTMAS DAY Sienna sat next to Kai and Kinny at a very long table in a room that opened to a veranda overlooking the lagoon on his grandparents' private island home. The rest of the table was filled with members of his extended family, including Uncle Rai and his wife and a number of other people who had been introduced as cousins. People were talking in a mixture of French and English, which she easily followed.

She had never imagined she could enjoy Christmas Day anywhere else but the family home in Chiswick, with her parents and sisters, but Christmas Day with Kai's family was exceeding all expectations. It was warm, inclusive, fun and she was treated as an honoured guest. She was with Kai and they didn't attempt to hide they were a couple—as if they hadn't all guessed anyway.

It was almost worth leaving home for Christmas to experience a day like this, she thought, and wondered what kind of Christmas her sisters were having in Japan and Costa Rica. She'd have loved to wish them and her parents Happy Christmas—or Joyeux Noel as they said here—in person, but the differing time zones made it too difficult. But she'd messaged them, knowing Thea had been the first to experience Christmas Day. She told them she'd been invited to join the family of her kitesurfing instructor, in that hospitable Polynesian way. If they wanted to guess there was something more to her friendship with her instructor, let them guess away.

Kai's parents Lana and Alain sat opposite them. His mother was a classic beauty, intelligent and articulate, his father tall, lean-faced, wearing glasses and fitting all her preconceived ideas about lawyers. They spoke perfect English and seemed surprised that she spoke French. She found it difficult to warm to them, knowing how they had rejected their son. But there didn't seem to be tension between parents and son, and she took her cues from Kai. She was surprised to see Alain interacting with Kinny. Kai told her Heiani had coached Kinny into saying Grandpapa Alain in the same way she'd taught her to say Sienna. Seemed Alain had fallen for the delightful little girl the same as everyone else had.

Her parents would love Kinny too.

The Christmas feast was a delicious mix of Polynesian and French, centring around roast turkey with chestnut stuffing, *dinde farcie aux marrons*. 'To please both you and the French family,' Kai said.

No plum pudding flaming with brandy for dessert, rather Buche de Noel, a log-shaped chocolate cake that Sienna had always preferred anyway, as well as the abundant fresh fruit that was one of the best things about her stay on Bora Bora.

Of course the very best thing about Bora Bora was meeting Kai. In fact, he might very well be the best thing that had ever happened to her in her life. She could not let him go. She would have to suggest they meet again. Kai travelled the world for Wave Hunters. He could surely meet her in London. Or she could meet him in Los Angeles. Perhaps they could have a holiday together. Vietnam, maybe, she'd always wanted to go there. He had business in Hanoi with a company that made their wetsuits, he'd told her. She'd have to speak up soon, as she was scheduled to leave the next morning, Boxing Day. The time to say goodbye was looming like the dark clouds that gathered before one of the tropical downpours that punctuated the day in this, what Kai called the wet season. But goodbye would be more bearable if she knew she would be seeing him again.

As the day progressed, she felt she never stopped talking and her mouth felt tired from smiling. Someone let slip that Kai had never brought a girlfriend to Christmas before; in fact, his private life was a mystery to his family. The advent of Kinny had apparently caused a real stir. She really liked both Kai's brothers and their wives. His two French nieces, Camille and Elodie, were charming, well mannered and too energetic to sit around. They did a good job keeping Kinny entertained and begged Uncle Kai to take them kitesurfing again. She never said more than hello to his nephew. He just wanted to play electronic games, much to the annoyance of his father.

After dessert, on some pretence, the nieces took her and Kai over to the entrance to the next room. Before they realised it, she and Kai were standing under a bunch of mistletoe. Of course they had to kiss and, once started, they didn't want to stop kissing, much to the delight of their audience. Pulling back from the kiss, flushed, laughing, still in the circle of Kai's arms, Sienna thought she had never had a more magical Christmas.

Kai wanted Sienna with him for this Christmas and every Christmas to come. She was perfect.

Not just for him, but for Kinny too. And his family loved her.

'Don't let her go. You'll regret it if you do,' his brother, Jules—conservative lawyer, the last person he expected to dish out advice on his love life—had warned him.

But he didn't need his brother's advice. Kai's gut instinct had never led him wrong, and it was screaming at him that Sienna was the one for him. He could not let Sienna go without securing her. Now was the moment, after that magical mistletoe kiss.

'Let's get some fresh air,' he said, steering her towards a private corner of the veranda, shaded by a ylang-ylang tree.

'That was such fun,' she said, her face flushed, eyes dancing. 'I really like your family.' She was wearing the pearl earrings she'd bought from Uncle Rai; a good omen, he thought.

'They really like you too. You're quite the hit of Christmas Day.'

'I actually think those two lovely nieces of yours are the hit of the day.'

'That's debatable,' he said. 'You'll always be the hit in my eyes.'

'Thank you,' she said softly. For a long moment she caught his gaze and he felt encouraged by the emotion he saw there.

'I have a Christmas present for you, but I

didn't want to give it to you in front of everyone.' He patted the pocket of his white linen shorts.

Sienna patted the pocket of her white full-skirted dress. 'Snap! I have one for you too.' She took out a small box, gift wrapped from Uncle Rai's shop, and handed it to him. 'I know you're a billionaire and all, so I didn't know what to get you that you wouldn't already have.'

'My favourite gift comes wrapped in a *pareo*,' he said huskily.

'That's the kind of present that pleases both giver and receiver,' she said with her slow, sensual smile. They shared a swift, sweet kiss.

He couldn't let her go.

'Go on, open it,' she urged.

Kai wasn't a man who cared to wear jewellery, but this twisted leather wristband with the black pearl and the silver clasp was something different. 'I like this very much. Thank you. I'll put it on.'

'Let me fasten it for you.' Her fingers were cool on his skin, her touch already so familiar and treasured. She snapped the clasp shut. 'There.'

He held up his hand for her to admire.

'It suits you. I'm so glad. I really didn't know what to get you.'

'I knew exactly what to get you,' he said. He

pulled the box out of his pocket. It was also gift wrapped by Uncle Rai's shop.

'You also shopped at Uncle Rai's?' She unwrapped it, opened the velvet box, stared at it, shook her head in disbelief, looked up at him. 'Oh, Kai. The green pearl choker.'

'It seemed as it was made for you, you had to have it,' he said. 'I went back and bought it that day.'

'You shouldn't have. It's too much,' she said. She reverently lifted up a strand, enough to finger one of the pearls. 'It's beyond beautiful.'

'The pearls looked so perfect on you. They really do reflect the colour of your eyes.' In his eyes, she was as rare and perfect as those prized green pearls.

Her green eyes were troubled. 'I don't have to tell you that I absolutely love this choker. I would have bought it myself if I could have. But—'

'No buts. You have to keep it. Uncle Rai has a no-returns policy.' He didn't. 'And it's way too big for Kinny.'

She smiled but it was a smile that didn't reach her eyes. 'You are too generous. You've been generous to me from the start. You know I don't want to say goodbye. I was wondering if we could—'

He put his hands on her shoulders subconsciously, perhaps, wanting to anchor her to him. 'Then don't go tomorrow, Sienna. Stay with me.'

Her eyes widened. 'Stay here?'

'Yes. Cancel your flight home.'

'Well, I could probably stay a few more days. I was going to suggest we see each other after I go back home, in London or somewhere else but—'

'I had in mind more than a few days. Live with me on Motu Puaiti. Get the house the way you want it. Make it your home.'

'Kai, I can't. There's my work.'

'Can't you post your social media from anywhere?'

'Not as an ongoing thing.'

'Isn't there some way you could make your business work by staying here with me?'

'No. My work is in London. I have to be on the spot for site meetings and to meet with clients and to keep up-to-date with trends and products. My identity as an influencer is as a Londoner.' She paused, then her voice hardened. 'Actually, Kai, I shouldn't need to explain myself when it comes to my business, my life.'

'I think we could have something lasting together.' This wasn't going the way he'd planned. But he had to keep on trying.

'I...I thought that too,' she said. 'But not—'

'I want you to stay. Or go home, sort things out

and come back to me. Plan a life together. You, me and Kinny. You know I can give you anything you want. Just ask.'

He just didn't get it.

Sienna was so disappointed she could hardly find the words to tell him that. She was thinking of them getting to know each other back in the real world. He was thinking…take over her life. She couldn't let that happen again. Is this why people warned against holiday romances? Did she really know him?

'Kai, this is too soon, too rushed.'
And all on his terms.

She was in love with him. Deeply in love with him. But that wasn't enough. She had to hold on to her plans, her life and be sure that someone else wasn't going to expect her to drop her dreams to suit their dreams. She'd made that mistake before and it wasn't going to happen again. No matter how much she loved this man—and his daughter. Heck, she'd fallen for his family too.

'Kai, I can't stay. I have to fly out of here as planned tomorrow. Don't try and stop me.'

'You know I wouldn't try to force you to do anything.'

'I know. But I have to go. Back to my life.'

'If that's what you really want.'

He sounded defeated and her heart wrenched with sadness about that. But she had to think of herself, protect her dreams, like she hadn't before in her disastrous marriage.

Without saying anything, Kai put his arm around her and pulled her close. She nestled against his shoulder, already so familiar.

She wanted him so much but it wasn't going to work.

She put up her hand to stop him saying anything to try to make her change her mind.

'Please don't make me cry, because I want to cry and I can't let myself,' she said, trying to keep her voice steady. 'This isn't the way I wanted things to end for us.'

'Hear that sniffing? That's me trying not to cry.'

'Oh, don't. You always know how to make me laugh.'

I love you, Kai, but it's too late to say it now.

She pulled away from him, gave an exaggerated sniff. 'Now that neither of us is crying, I need for you to walk around with me while I say goodbye to your family and thank your grandparents for the most marvellous Christmas. If they ask when they'll see me again, we can say something like, *soon, I hope* and leave it at that without committing to anything. Then, without making a big deal about it, I'd like you to take me back to the resort. The shuttle boat transport is booked to take me to the airport on Motu Mute early in the morning.'

'Will I see you again?'

She took a deep breath. This was the most difficult thing she had ever had to do.

'Soon, I hope.'

The boat trip back to Mareva was awkward and spent mostly in silence. Kai had never felt more rejected and miserable—even when his parents had booted him out of home. What more was there for him or Sienna to say? He walked her to her villa, where they had so recently spent such a happy time, and formally wished her a safe journey home. She tried to give him back the green pearl choker but he wouldn't take it. It meant too much. When she insisted, he told her he would toss it over the deck for the sharks and stingrays to play with and she'd half-laughed, half-cried and agreed to keep it.

When he got back home, there were still some guests sitting and chatting. He went in search of his grandmother. She was supervising the maids clearing the big table. 'Can I help, Mama'u?'

She frowned. 'Where is Sienna?'

'Gone.'

'What do you mean *gone*? I thought she would be staying here with you tonight.'

'She's flying back home tomorrow morning and thought it would be easier to go from Mareva.'

'What did you say to drive her away?'

'Nothing. I tried to keep her here.'

He told her what had happened.

'You silly boy,' she scolded.

At thirty-five years old, Kai's grandmother was the only person he would allow to call him a *silly boy* and that not very often—this time he thought perhaps he deserved it.

'Sienna told me some of her history,' his grandmother said. 'That horrible first husband who was obviously jealous of her because she was smarter and more talented than he was. How he did everything he could to drag her down out of spite and trampled on her dreams just because he could. You told her you could give her anything she wanted, but what she really wants is the autonomy and independence she had to fight hard to claw back. The last thing she wants is a man who starts to lay down the law about where she will live and what she will do with her highly successful career.'

'That wasn't what I meant at all,' Kai said. He groaned. 'I knew how fragile she was when it came to that, how she needed support and nurturing. The words came out wrong because I so badly wanted her in my life. I love her, Mama'u.'

'Get after her and tell her that, *show* her that. What's keeping you tied to Bora Bora anyway that she should give up everything to come here?'

'You and Papa'u…Kinny.'

'We'd be poor grandparents if we expected you to live with us forever, in spite of our ties of kinship. As an adult you never spent much time here before we were blessed with Kinny. We've always encouraged you to follow your dreams, and look at the soaring success you've found away from here. Kinny needs to be brought up by her father—not her great-grandparents. You realise Kinny knows that Sienna should be her mother? She knows, you know, I know, and I suspect Sienna knows.'

'You wouldn't mind if I took Kinny away to live elsewhere?'

'As long as you brought her back to visit as often as you could. I get feelings, intuition— what you call gut instinct. Kinny gets them, too, though she's too young to recognise them yet.'

'She took to Sienna immediately.'

'As soon as I met Sienna, I knew she was the one for you. She should be your wife and a mother to Kinny. You both know that to be the truth but are scared of it—Sienna because it seems too soon after her divorce, you because you've never made a commitment to a woman before and don't know how.'

'That's harsh,' he said, frowning.

'Look closely and you'll see I'm right. You've been used to running your own show without much compromise and you need to learn to compromise for a happy relationship. You can brave the face of Teahupoo. Don't let pride stop you from winning a very special young woman who loves you as much as you love her. Go let her know you want her—on her terms. It doesn't matter that you've only known her ten days. When you know, you know.'

'I'll take Kinny with me.'

His grandmother's face split into a big smile. 'I'll pack a bag for Kinny tomorrow.'

CHAPTER SIXTEEN

BACK IN LONDON, Sienna was having trouble sleeping. She was alone in the Chiswick house, except for her cat, Lucky, who lay curled up on her bed between her feet. She didn't miss her parents and her sisters. They'd be back soon so they could all spend New Year's Eve together.

She missed Kai.

She'd been back two days and she missed him with an aching yearning that physically hurt.

She'd gone over and over that final scene. But no matter how many times she did, she knew she would do the same thing again—although she hated that she had hurt Kai. She could not, would not, have history repeat itself and end up in the same powerless place she'd ended up in with Callum.

What she should have done sooner was suggest to Kai that they meet again once she got home and look seriously at how they could move forward into a relationship. Then he mightn't have felt he'd have to lay down the terms he had, terms that seemed so out of character with the man she'd come to know and love. But best to be forewarned.

The flight home had been miserable. It was such a long way and only served to underscore that she couldn't run her business from Tahiti. When she'd got back to London it had been sleeting and grey and it had been difficult for her to believe Bora Bora and London actually coexisted on the same planet. She tried to imagine herself back in those warm, aquamarine waters swimming with turtles and a beautiful man, but it wouldn't work. Had it all been just a fantasy?

Her video posts proved that it had been only too real. In a gloomy Northern Hemisphere winter, her images of an island paradise so beautiful as to seem otherworldly had had a good response. The wooden toy cooperative had been inundated with orders. A favourite client was delighted that those stylish bamboo chairs she'd fallen for at the beach bar that first night were on their way from the workshop that made them via express freight to the client's new conservatory in Surrey. But she hadn't posted Uncle Rai's pearls yet. That was simply too close to Kai. And she would never share an image of her green pearl choker that sat unworn in its velvet box.

She'd had another restless night, haunted by

dreams of Kai. Her dream had taken a cruel twist to let her know he wasn't real and she'd woken with her cheeks wet with tears. The central heating had kicked in not long ago and she was waiting in bed for the house to get toastier. The doorbell rang. It was two flights of stairs down and she decided to ignore it. It rang again, more urgently. Parcel delivery probably.

'All right, all right,' she grumbled, slipping into her ancient dressing gown she kept here— most of her clothes were in storage until she bought her own place—and the fluffy kitten slippers with the googly eyes Eliza had given her.

'Coming, coming,' she called as she headed down the stairs, stifling a yawn.

She peered through the spyhole and stilled, shocked. Kinny's little face looked through at her. She fumbled with the bolts and chain in her haste to open the door, which only slowed her down. At last, she got the door open. There was Kai, looking city-smart elegant in a beautifully tailored black cashmere coat and holding Kinny in his arms. He had Kinny's nappy bag slung over his shoulder, an incongruous accessory for Savile Row tailoring.

Sienna's heart thudded so loudly she was sure he must hear it, and she had to clutch on to the door frame for support. 'Kai, come in. It's bitter out there.'

Kinny held out her arms. 'Sienna,' she said.

Sienna's heart turned over. She took her from Kai. 'Come here, sweetheart, you've got a lovely padded jacket and trousers on, but it's warmer inside. You're not used to this kind of weather.' She turned to Kai. 'What are you doing here?'

'We've come to see you, if that's not stating the obvious.' Despite his bold words there was a note of uncertainty to his deep, husky voice.

'I'm glad to see you, if that's not stating the obvious.' She looked up at him, over his baby daughter's head, knowing her heart must be showing in her eyes. 'I...I've missed you so much.' That's not what she'd planned to say if she'd ever seen him again. But it was what she meant.

'I miss you too.' His voice was hoarse with longing and she realised he'd probably been as miserable without her as she'd been without him.

She was suddenly lost for words. 'Get your coat off and hang it on the rack there,' she said briskly, to hide her confusion. The entrance hallway suddenly seemed crowded with Kai's height and broad shoulders. 'Come into the kitchen. Coffee? Tea? And what about Kinny?'

'Coffee for me. There's food for Kinny in the bag and a sippy-cup. Let me look after her while you make coffee. We've come straight from the airport.'

'Good idea.'

She caught sight of herself in the hallway mirror and shrieked. 'Oh, my gosh, what am I wearing? This is ancient. I should have thrown it out years ago. And my hair!'

Kai grinned, that big, familiar grin. 'You look lovely. You always do. And I think Kinny will really like the cat slippers.'

'Not to mention a real cat. She's upstairs. She's just like the cat in her little train.'

Sienna made coffee for two and sat opposite him on her parents' round kitchen table, still scarcely able to believe he was here. Kinny sat on Kai's lap, sucking her thumb, her eyes heavy and drowsy. 'She didn't sleep on the plane,' he said.

'That must have been fun for you.'

'Yup. And one thing they don't love in first class is a baby. We stopped over in LA, but her sleep patterns are completely disrupted.'

She held the silence between them for a beat. 'Kai, why are you here?'

He didn't hesitate. 'To tell you that I love you.'

'Oh.' She paused, shocked, warmed, happy, at the sincerity of his words. 'I...I love you, too, so much,' she said, glad to finally put voice to her feelings. 'But that doesn't change things. I don't want to live in Bora Bora. Visit, yes. Live, no.'

'And I was an idiot to ask you to. I'm sorry. I was just so overjoyed at having you with me on

Christmas Day—that's the first Christmas Day where I haven't wanted to walk out before the turkey was even served. You made all the difference. I knew you were leaving in the morning and I wanted to secure you. I went about it entirely the wrong way.'

'Yes, you did,' she said, wondering where this could possibly be going.

'I don't ever want to hold you back from your dreams, especially to further mine. My brand is global. I can work from anywhere. Your career is strongly rooted in London. I want to live where you live, wherever that might be. My… My heart is with you. If you plan to live in London, so do I.' He paused. 'This is difficult for me to say.'

'Keep going, I'm loving what you're saying.' She noticed he was wearing the black wristband she had given him.

'Travel is an important part of my work. There's no avoiding it. But I could sell off one of the divisions of the company, which would level the load a bit.'

'Would you want to do that?'

'Not really. Not yet. But if it would make life easier for you—that is assuming you wanted to link your life with mine—I would do it.'

Did she want to link her life with his? Yes, she did. A few days away from him had told her that. But there were a few answers she needed first before she committed to anything. 'What about Kinny?'

'Kinny and I come as a package deal. Where I live, she lives.'

'As it should be. If we…link lives as you say…would I be her mother?'

'Yes. Without a doubt, yes.'

Kinny started to snore, little baby snores. Sienna looked at Kai. He rolled his eyes and laughed. 'She does that,' he said.

'It's not because of the cold air? It must be quite a shock for her coming from Tahiti's sunny climate.'

'No, it could be because of the air in the plane cabin but probably not.'

'Why don't we move her into the living room?' she said. 'Us too.'

Kai stood up with a sleeping Kinny in his arms, and Sienna led him into the living room. 'How about I make a little nest of cushions for her on the sofa, and barricade her in so she can't roll off?'

'Let me help.'

Sienna settled herself on the sofa next to Kai, with Kinny next to him.

Like a family.

'Poor little thing is out like a light,' she said. She looked up into his face. 'I love her, too, you know.'

'I know.'

'I've so desperately wanted a child. It's what I've wanted for years, what I've always wanted. Kinny feels like that child. I know it's irrational, but there was something about her that called to me, the same thing about you that called to me, that makes me love you when I've only known you for two weeks. Oddly, I think Kinny felt it too. I saw a…a recognition in her eyes that I don't think I was imagining.'

'I don't think you were imagining it, either. She knows.'

'I want to be able to tell people she's my daughter, not hide that Paige is her birth mother, but that I'm her mother now. I don't want Kinny to be known as Kai's daughter and me as her stepmother. That means shared parenting, shared decisions.'

'It will be good to have you share all that with me. It can get difficult on your own.'

'Of course I have to learn to be a mother. I really don't have a clue, except I want what's best for her.'

'That's a good place to start. It's where I started.'

'And look what a great dad you've turned out to be,' she said.

'I could be a good dad to other children, too, if that's what you wanted.'

'You'd want more children?' she said, holding her breath for his answer.

'If you do,' he said. 'I'd like a bigger family.'

She let out her breath on a sigh of happiness. 'If that happened, I'd be ecstatic. But having a baby with you wouldn't make me love Kinny less.'

'I know that… Me neither,' he said. 'But I missed out on her first six months, on her mother's pregnancy. I'd like to experience that, if we were blessed with a baby.'

She leaned over to kiss him, something she'd been longing to do since she saw him at the door. Every minute away from him had been hell. 'How come you're saying all the right things now, when you were so wrong back then?'

'Time spent in misery without you? Also thinking, really thinking, about everything you'd told me about your life, and how you wanted things now.'

'Now he says even more of the right things,' she said with a watery smile. Having let her guard down she felt close to tears.

'I mean every word and will grovel about those wrong words.'

'I never want to hear you grovel. Not to me, not to anyone. That's not Kai Hunter.'

'Thank you.'

'I have to be careful. I committed my life

to the wrong man once and I don't want to do that again.'

'You can be confident I am the right man.'

In her heart, she was absolutely sure of that too.

'Coming back to Kinny,' Kai said. 'I would like to take her sometimes to visit her family in Bora Bora, especially her great-grandparents.'

'Yes, they love her so much. That would be essential. I think your parents would want to see her too. There will be school holidays for Kinny before we know it. And the surf and the water will be there for you too. I know how much you need it.'

'There's a house on Motu Puaiti that needs refurbishing.'

'The one with six new bathrooms required?'

'That's the one. It could become a home for when we visit,' he said.

'It could also be a project for me. A room-by-room renovation conducted online. You know how much I love that house. And…and the memories we made there.' She remembered making love under the stars, swimming naked in the sea, the awakening of her true sensuality. And a very different but magical Christmas.

'We can make those memories anywhere,' he said.

She looked up into his eyes. 'You would actually do all this for me?'

'For us. For our London base, I'm thinking of a big house with a garden, with easy access to Heathrow.'

'And not far from Chiswick,' she said.

'I know how important your family is to you. We should live nearby.'

She frowned. 'This is all very theoretical.'

'It's up to you to put it into practice. When you're ready.'

'What do you mean?'

'Where is the nappy bag?'

'In the kitchen. Does she need it?'

'I need something from out of it. I'll go get it.' He came back with a small box engraved with Uncle Rai's shop logo. He opened it to reveal a ring with a large central emerald surrounded by diamonds.

'Wow! Is that—?'

'Yes, it's an engagement ring. But I'm not going to rush you. I'm going to give this ring to you now to put somewhere safe. When you're ready, you can ask me to marry you.'

'That's a plan,' she said, not sure what to make of this unusual proposal—if indeed that was what it was.

'I'm ready now, just so you know,' he said. 'To marry you, I mean.'

'Really?'

For the first time she saw him disconcerted. 'Yes. I want to be your husband.'

'Because so am I. Ready, I mean. I want to be your wife and a mother to Kinny.' She took a deep breath. 'Will you marry me, Kai?'

He smiled that wonderful smile that had so captivated her when she first saw him kitesurfing. 'Yes,' he said. 'I will marry you and cherish you and love you.'

She had to blink back sudden tears of joy. 'I will cherish and love you too.'

'Let me put the ring on your finger,' he said.

The magnificent emerald slipped on easily. 'It's a perfect fit,' she said, holding out her hand and splaying her fingers to show it off. 'It's utterly gorgeous.' Little tremors of excitement and hope ran through her.

'Thanks to Uncle Rai. Do you remember you tried on some pearl rings? He recorded your size then.'

'Did he? How did he know…? Never mind.'

She kissed him; she could never remember being so happy and so certain about the future. 'Do you remember when I wished upon the shooting star?'

'Yes.'

'I wished for a second chance to live my dreams. Then I made a second wish on a second star and I wished that second chance would be with you.'

'Powerful wishing stars must have been flying through the universe that night. Because my wish came true too.'

'What did you wish?'

'I wished that Sienna Kendall would fall in love with me.'

'And I did,' she said, kissing him again.

* * * * *

Look out for the next story in
The Christmas Pact trilogy

Cinderella's Costa Rican Adventure
by Scarlet Wilson

And if you enjoyed this story,
check out these other great reads
from Kandy Shepherd

Pregnancy Shock for the Greek Billionaire
Second Chance with His Cinderella
From Bridal Designer to Bride

All available now!